The SEAL's
Best Man

SPECIAL OPS: HOMEFRONT

Kate Aster

Cover Design and Interior format by The Killion Group
http://thekilliongroupinc.com

DEDICATION

This book is dedicated to every reader of SEAL the Deal *with my thanks for your reviews, support, and encouragement to write Maeve and Jack's story. Thank you.*

PART ONE

Eight years ago

"*Call me,*" *he said, slipping a piece of paper into her hand.*

His hands moved to her waist and she could feel the ripples of his abs against her as he pulled her snug against his body. A white t-shirt covered his torso. It was worn and thin, only suitable for underneath a uniform. But as unshaven as he was, he joked he'd get court-martialed if anyone saw him like this while wearing his Navy whites.

The threadbare cotton hugged tight to his broad pecs and the short sleeves showed off a set of biceps that looked like they were sculpted by the hand of God. The pants from his uniform hung low on his waist, taut against the subtle bulge at his crotch that even now tempted her.

He should have looked like the milkman, all dressed in white—not the least bit enticing at all. But instead he looked like a creamy vanilla ice cream cone that was meant to be licked.

Maeve swallowed, holding back the impulse to rip his t-shirt from his body and explore every square inch of him... again.

His lips touched hers, tenderly this time, not the searing passion that they had shared the first time they had sex when she had shattered unapologetically with him inside her. Or the second time. Or the... well, she had lost count somewhere around twelve.

It was sweet, aching tenderness she felt from him now, the kind of honeyed warmth that almost—almost—had her considering programming his number into her cell phone.

But she wouldn't. Even as her mouth opened to him, tasting him one last time, she knew she couldn't call. His hands locked behind her neck, as his mouth devoured her, making every cell of her body spring to life and reminding her how she could have invited him—a man she had just met— into her grandparents' house.

And into their bed, she thought in horror, her stomach clenching at the idea just as he released her from the kiss. She had been here in Annapolis to house-sit for them this weekend. Not to pick up a Naval Academy grad at a commencement party and discover new ways to use the whipped cream they had stashed in their fridge.

She blushed at the recollection. What would her beloved Gram think, if she ever found out what her granddaughter had done in that bed? And on the sofa. And kitchen table. And... who would have known the rhythm of a clothes washer underneath her could be so erotic?

"Call me," he had said, his uniform shirt casually flung over his arm and a confident smile on his face. Even as she watched him shut the door behind him, she knew she couldn't. She

crumpled the piece of paper in her hand and stood above the wastebasket, waiting to drop it in. Waiting... longer than she should have, as she toyed with it in her hand.

Jack wasn't part of her plan. Most of her friends from high school were married by now, a fact her mother reminded her of regularly. Maeve finally had her college degree in hand, a few internships under her belt, and had just been invited for a second interview at a major design firm in Baltimore.

At 29 years old, the life she wanted was just beginning.

She couldn't waste time on a new Navy officer who was headed to Rhode Island today, and then off to sea for who knows how long. No matter how great the sex was. No matter how fascinating the conversation. No matter how strong the connection.

"Destiny sometimes needs a push," her grandmother always told her. And Maeve was ready to push—as hard as she needed to—to get to where she had wanted to be since she had looked at her first book of swatches and color tiles at twelve years old.

Her destiny was in Baltimore, working the job of her dreams, settling down with a man in a suit who could come home to her at night. Not a man in uniform.

She unwrinkled the paper a moment, glancing down at it as she walked into the kitchen. No. She ripped it into tiny pieces this time, her hands shaking.

Turning to the kitchen sink, she dropped them down the drain and flicked on the disposal. The sound of the motor chopping them to bits should have comforted her, making her feel powerful and in control of her own destiny. Instead, it broke her heart.

He was a weekend fling. That's all he ever would be.

But one thing was clear:

Ensign Jack Falcone had ruined her for other men.

CHAPTER 1

Eight years later

She hated stilettos.

So maybe it was years of pent-up loathing that caused Maeve to liberate her aching feet and toss her pair of Jimmy Choos out of her BMW convertible as she raced down I-97 toward Annapolis.

Or maybe it was symbolic—her right shoe representing her boss as she sent it on an airborne path to certain doom on the pavement. The left one, her boss's lover, who was right now celebrating being added as the newest partner in the design firm where Maeve had slaved away for years.

Or maybe it was insanity. Because damn, those were expensive shoes.

Bare foot pressing the accelerator, she felt somehow calmed by the soothing roar of German engineering.

That partnership was meant to be hers, especially after snagging three of the highest profile clients the firm had ever enjoyed. But thanks to a non-compete clause in the contract she had signed years ago, her clients were now theirs. Her precious portfolio, lovingly created, would still appear on their website. And she was jobless, pressing her foot harder against the accelerator as she raced toward home.

Glancing behind her in the rear view mirror, her eyes spotted a cop two cars behind her, and she tapped the brakes lightly as she exited. Certainly couldn't afford a ticket right now, and she wasn't up to flirting with an officer to get out of it.

At a stoplight, her toes enjoyed the freedom, wiggling, waiting for the green that would bring her closer to home. Why did she always wear skyscraper heels? Why did she always have perfect hair and nails, and wear outfits that made her look like she should be traipsing down Beverly Hills' Rodeo Drive rather than Main Street, Annapolis, Maryland?

Why was she such a fake?

Approaching the Navy Memorial Bridge, a breath of Bay-scented air consoled her as she was greeted by the sweeping profile of the United States Naval Academy on the shore and sailboats on the Severn River enjoying an evening race. Having lived in many cities along the East Coast, Annapolis was easily the most appealing.

Her eyes drifted to one of the many reasons: a group of Naval Academy men, instructors in the early thirties by her appraisal, on their evening run across the bridge. She sighed appreciatively.

Behind them, a group of Midshipmen ran, their fresh, young faces reminding Maeve of the many summers she had stayed in Annapolis with her grandparents as a teenager. Too many times to count, she had borrowed her Grandmother's red VW beetle and taken a leisurely drive, playfully tapping her horn and waving at the appealing college men. She had been such a flirt in high school, and an innocent one at that. But with the killer looks to back it up.

Feeling remarkably calmer, she pulled into her driveway, noticing the usual assortment of cars in front of her humble Cape Cod.

Mick's SUV and Jack's truck were pulled along the curb. It was a full house tonight, which could only mean one thing: Bess was cooking.

Even as Maeve thought it, the smell of something wonderful wafted her way through the house's open windows towards Maeve's convertible. Garlic and—what was it? Basil perhaps?

Maeve wasn't the culinary genius her housemate Bess was, but she was enough of a gourmet to appreciate a fine meal. As she turned off her car, her stomach instinctively grumbled.

Tiptoeing on her bare feet up the sun-blasted cement, she briefly considered doing a 180 and going back to search for her discarded shoes somewhere near the Odenton exit. There was still a chance they hadn't been destroyed by oncoming traffic or snatched up by a fellow size 8 who had damn good taste.

But the thought of an awaiting sunset on her back deck, and a nice glass of Pinot tugged her up her front steps.

She was home. Her sanctuary. And right now, a quiet evening with her friends was exactly what she needed. Some genuine sympathy and a good meal.

She stepped into the house unnoticed, the click of the doorknob drowned out by the sizzle of frying chicken and laughter. Maeve stood in silence a moment and let the comfort of being surrounded by her friends fill her.

Bess stood behind the stove, the only place where Maeve saw her move with swift confidence. She was dressed in her usual blue sweats with her lustrous red hair hidden in a tight ponytail.

She saw her other housemate Lacey, sitting at the kitchen table, pouring a bowl of fluffy mashed potatoes into a baking dish. Her mannerisms were so contented these days with a hefty diamond on her ring finger. Her fiancé, Mick, stood behind her, his hand on her shoulder so naturally, it was as though he couldn't be within a foot of his fiancée without touching her. It made Maeve smile.

Maeve approached them, but before her first foot fell to the tiled floor of the kitchen, she was swept into a romantic dip, seeing nothing but the ceiling and two eyes the color of the Ireland's emerald coastline.

Before she could even register Jack's body pressed against hers, she felt his breath tickle her lips with his face so close to hers. She inhaled sharply from the shock, taking in his slightly soapy scent mixed with a hint of Sam Adams.

Captivating grin firmly in place, his hand tightly cradled her back, while the other ventured gently up the skin of her neck, pausing slightly as though to detect her rapid-fire pulse. His touch was electric, sending shivers down her spine.

The moment couldn't have lasted more than a second or two before he spoke, his breath intermingling with hers, igniting an unexpected fire inside her that toasted her down to her bare, pedicured toes.

"Beautiful, are you tired?" he asked, in a voice she hardly recognized.

Even as she struggled to comprehend his words, Maeve couldn't resist sliding her hand along the front of his chest on a muscle-rippled path to his sculpted shoulders. Breathless, she only managed to respond, "Huh?"

"Because you've been running through my dreams all night."

A gagging sound came from somewhere in the kitchen, and Jack raised an eyebrow in the direction of the sound.

Bess was the source. "*That's* the best you can do?"

Holding a beer in his firm grip, Mick shook his head. "Better brush up on your pick-up lines, Jack, or you'll be the first best man in history to go home alone after a wedding."

"I like the dip, though." Lacey's grin was wistful. "Nice touch."

Baffled and uncomfortably steamy beneath her sheath dress, Maeve struggled to snap back to reality. "Anyone care to clue me in about what you're all talking about?"

Jack's eyes were full of laughter as he set Maeve to rights, two feet on the ground. "The best man is always supposed to hit on the bridesmaids. Haven't you been to any weddings?"

"Plenty. Including my own." Still reeling, Maeve found herself unable to meet his eyes. For a moment in his arms so brief, the effects registered 7.9 on the Richter scale. "Our best man went home with my maid of honor after one-too-many shots."

Jack waggled his eyebrows. "I should be so lucky. Lacey's sister is hot as hell."

"And married," Bess warned. "You'd never." She flipped the chicken in front of her and did a double-take over her shoulder at Maeve. "Oh my God. Are you blushing, Maeve?"

Blushing was an understatement. Half the blood in her body had rushed to her cheeks and the other half rushed… someplace much farther South. It was hard enough tolerating Jack Falcone's unplanned re-emergence into her life after they had bumped into each other at O'Toole's one night out with her housemates.

But now that *his* friend, Mick, was engaged to *her* friend, Lacey, there was no avoiding him.

Not that she'd tried too hard. After all, what girl could resist having a set of pecs like his around her house from time to time? But if she were to maintain his friendship—strictly friendship—then Jack had to adhere to her stringent hands-off policy.

A girl only has so much self-control.

Lightly touching her cheeks, Maeve protested. "I am not blushing. I had the top down on the convertible and probably got too much sun." Maeve's eyes darted to Lacey and Mick. "And what is he talking about? Best man for what?"

Hands entwined with her fiancé, Lacey glowed. "Mick and I finally set a date for the wedding. And we'd like you and Bess to be bridesmaids. I asked my sister to be maid of honor."

Despite her escalated body temperature, Maeve managed a smile. "You know I'd love to. So when are you doing it?" She stepped away from Jack, hoping he didn't notice the trickle of perspiration on her brow. Why *was* her body responding to him this way? She wasn't sixteen. She'd been held by plenty of men. But, God help her, his arms were honed from granite.

Lacey bit her lip. "Six weeks from tomorrow."

That was enough to snap Maeve back to reality. "Six weeks? You can't plan a wedding in six weeks." She stepped toward her. "Oh my God. Are you pregnant?" Wavering, she found herself balanced by Jack's sturdy presence behind her.

"No. Mick got the orders he was hoping for. He's headed to the SEALs in Coronado in two months. We're delaying the honeymoon till we've moved to San Diego. That'll be an easier flight to Hawaii, anyway."

"Honeymoon in Hawaii?" Bess let out a squeal.

Lacey's hand traced Mick's arm affectionately. "We'll just do something small—you know, at City Hall with you guys, our families, and a few others."

Maeve's eyes bugged out. "City Hall? No, no, no. Lacey, you need a real wedding. White gown, bouquets, overcooked chicken, drunken guests." She finally set down her keys and purse on the kitchen table, grateful that no one had noticed her missing shoes. Now was definitely not the time to share her bad news.

Lacey laughed. "There's no time. And I'm fine with it. I'd rather use the money for a down payment on a house."

"A house?"

Lacey pressed her lips together and smiled. "Can you believe it? I'm finally going to own a house of my own. We're headed out west in a few weeks to look at some properties. Finally I won't be the only real estate agent who doesn't own real estate."

"A house? That's so—wonderful." And permanent, Maeve thought, her smile frozen in place. She had known it would happen. From the moment Mick and Lacey got engaged, Lacey had told her an eventual move to Naval Base Coronado was in their plans. But actually buying a house?

At the reality of losing her best friend, she swallowed a half-sob, and masked it in feigned happiness. "I'm so happy for you," she said, hugging her a little tighter than usual at the thought of her friend being a full continent away. "But City Hall? We have to do *something*, Lacey. You only do this once. Well, theoretically."

Pulling a spoon from the drawer, Jack shrugged. "Words falling on deaf ears, Maeve. Bess and I have been telling them that for almost an hour now." He stole a taste of the gravy on the stove and received a firm slap on the hand from Bess in rebuke.

Lacey shrugged. "No one can pull off a wedding in six weeks."

"I can," Maeve said firmly, trying to convince herself as much as them.

"And in June? Everything will be booked solid."

Mick rested one hand on his fiancée's shoulder and touched her cheek affectionately. "We don't need to rush it. I don't want you having regrets."

Maeve stepped back instinctively, feeling as though she was intruding on their private moment, and she felt Jack's hand lightly touch her back behind her.

She stiffened. As a friend, he had made this simple gesture a thousand times since he had come back into her life almost two years ago. Yet somehow tonight his touch made half the air escape her lungs. She swallowed, and dared to meet his eyes.

He grinned at her. "If Maeve says she can plan a wedding in six weeks, she can."

Maeve warmed. After such a bad day at work, it was nice to know someone had confidence in her skills. Her eyes met his for a brief moment and the connection seemed magnetic, before he snuck behind Bess for another sample of gravy.

Why was she reacting to Jack this way?

It must be the effects of being jobless. She was simply feeling vulnerable. That's what it was, she assured herself. It was perfectly natural to be drawn to the first strong presence she encountered. As he turned away from her to sneak a spoonful of potatoes, her eyes drifted over his broad, muscled back appraisingly.

And what a fine presence he was.

Barely withholding a purr, she turned her attention back to Lacey. "It doesn't take much to throw a wedding. You'll still have money for a down payment. I can do it on a budget."

Bess laughed. "This, coming from a woman who's never worked on a budget in her life."

"I'll pitch in," Jack said. "You'll need a Navy guy to figure out the Navy stuff. You know, sword arches and all that."

"I'll help too," Bess chimed in just as she heard her baby start wailing in the distance. Having just turned a year old, little Abigail's naps were getting shorter every day. Bess set down her spatula. "Well, I'll help when *she* lets me. Can someone watch this? I think there's a diaper with my name on it."

"I'll get this one," Jack offered.

Maeve's eyes couldn't resist following him as his long strides took him out of the kitchen on a mission. There was something undeniably sexy about a man who looked like *that*—and was willing to take on diaper duty.

"I don't know..." Lacey sank into a kitchen chair, a sign to Maeve that her resolve was crumbling.

Maeve moved in for the kill, feeling her old self again with Jack out of the room. "No arguments. We'll talk about it over dinner. Make a few calls. All I need is a head count. The rest is easy."

And it could be easy, she convinced herself. Weddings didn't have to be the extravaganza that she had barely survived. Her wedding had been filled with as much drama as her subsequent divorce.

For Lacey, it would be classy. Simple and elegant. A celebration of love. Maeve smiled, picturing her best friend and closest confidant in a flowing white gown, eyes filled with hope.

Despite the loss of her job, Maeve actually felt a small surge of excitement… until Jack walked back into the kitchen, cradling a baby against his chest.

And Maeve's heart broke from the glimpse of an impossible future.

Swallowing the lump in her throat, she dared to meet his eyes. "Umm, Jack, do you think we could get the Navy Chapel?"

"You'll never get it. That place gets booked up a year in advance."

As he bent to set Abigail in her playpen, Maeve couldn't help noticing how his uniform showed off his perfect butt. Couldn't the guy have some flaw she could focus on right now? She sighed. "But Mick's a freaking war hero. Can't they bump someone for us?"

Lacey and Jack exchanged a look.

Maeve rolled her eyes. "Okay, okay. Bad idea. We can count out any of the churches downtown, too. Anyplace historic will be taken that month. What about Eagle's Point?"

"On our budget? Are you kidding? That would eat up our down payment before we even cut the cake. Besides, I guarantee their ballroom will be booked up every Saturday in June."

"True." Maeve deleted Eagle's Point from the list she was already tapping into her iPhone. "I do like the waterfront twist though. How about at Edith's house?" Maeve knew there was little that Edith Baker would not do for Mick. She and her late husband had been his sponsors at the Academy his plebe year. She was still a mother hen to him.

Mick shook his head. "I wouldn't want to put her out like that."

Setting down her phone, Maeve sighed. "She'd love it. You know she would."

Lacey piped in. "Can't do it there anyway. Edith's neighborhood has too many covenants. It would have to get approved by the Homeowners' Association and that would never happen in time."

Glancing out her window, Maeve eyed her backyard. It certainly wasn't the size of Edith's—which practically qualified for its own zip code. But maybe... "What about here?"

"Here?" Biting her lip, Lacey stood to look out the back window.

"Yeah. I could fire cannons off the back porch and no one would care in our community. And you probably don't want a huge wedding anyway, right, Lacey? I mean, how many people are we talking?"

"It's up to Lacey," Mick said, resting his arm low around his fiancée's waist.

"Not true, Mick." Jack grabbed a stack of plates from the cupboard. "You're in the Navy.

Navy lists get big fast. You invite one person from a wardroom, and you have to invite them all. This place will be crawling with SEALs."

Maeve raised her eyebrows. *Crawling with SEALs?* She could sell tickets to single women in Annapolis and finance Lacey's entire honeymoon from it.

Bess narrowed her eyes on the grin spreading across Maeve's face. "Don't even say it, Maeve."

Wide-eyed, Maeve protested, "What?"

Mick pulled out silverware and followed Jack onto the back porch. "It won't be as bad as that. Most the people I know will be OCONUS in June."

"OCONUS?" Maeve set down the napkins. "Mind a translation for us mere civilians?"

"Outside the Continental U.S." He laid out the forks and knives alongside the plates.

Maeve took Lacey by the hand and guided her out the door of the screened porch. "Picture it, Lacey. It's flat right there by the water's edge. We can rent a dance floor and put it down there. Put chairs on it for the ceremony." Excited now, she touched her fingers to her lips and thoughtfully gazed back at her house. "Then we could have guests retreat to the house for cocktail hour, while someone whisks away the chairs and sets up tables off to the side for dinner."

Jack darted back up the stairs of the porch and turned to them. "I'm thinking we could do the sword arch here, and then you'd walk down to the dance floor for your first dance."

Lacey clasped Mick's hand. "That would be beautiful."

"It'll be a breeze. I'll have help from Bess and—Jack." Maeve nearly sputtered his name, wondering what it would be like to plan a wedding with a man who was, right now, sending her hormones into overdrive. "Let me do this for you. It won't be lavish, but any wedding we throw for you will beat City Hall. Do you want us to?"

Lacey released her fiancé to hug Maeve. "I do."

Maeve grinned. "Good practice."

The clock had said it was just past midnight, but Maeve felt like it was barely seven o'clock. She couldn't sleep; hadn't even bothered trying. Instead of counting sheep, she'd be counting unpaid bills in her head—gas, electric, cell phone, cable—and wondering where the money would come from.

Her house, inherited from her grandmother two years ago, didn't generate anything more than a tax bill twice a year. But still, taxes for waterfront property in Annapolis were grueling. Worth every penny though, she was reminded as she stepped out the door from her screened-in back porch to the yard. Tilting her neck back, she drank in the sight of the stars above her.

A breeze caught her nightgown and she cuddled it closer to her body as she walked onto her wooden dock. It was a perfect May night, and she could easily spend the next hour or two just soaking in the warm spring breeze that hinted of the summer that still awaited her. The moon's reflection in the water drew her eyes upward again to the calming presence of the stars. Twinkling their light down upon the house, Maeve sometimes thought of her beloved Gram up there, still watching over her granddaughter now, just as she had in life.

"What are you doing out here?"

Maeve's heart jumped in her chest at the sound of Jack's voice behind her.

"Jack, you scared me." Instinctively, she wrapped her arms across her chest. "I didn't know you were still here."

"Abigail fell asleep in my arms. I was afraid if I put her down, she'd wake up."

"Liar. You just love holding her."

"Caught." He stepped onto the dock. "Truth be known, I fell asleep in the rocker holding her. Nothing makes me sleepier than having a warm baby snoozing on my chest. All these nieces and nephews I have, and I kept missing the chance to really enjoy them when they were babies." Joining her at the end of the dock, he sat down, his feet nearly touching the water below him. "She's out like a light in her crib now, though." He brushed off the boards of the dock beside him. "Why don't you sit?"

Maeve shook her head. "My robe's too thin. I'll be picking splinters out of my thighs."

Jack laughed. "Well, we can't have that." He pulled his shirt off and spread it out on the dock beside him.

Maeve just stood there, slack-jawed, wondering how a mere crescent moon could give off enough light to showcase such a perfect torso.

"Might want to put that shirt back on. The water is beginning to boil around you."

Jack tilted his head. "A rare compliment from you. I'll have to mark this day in my calendar."

Maeve gave in and sat on the shirt beside him. She noticed how it was still warm from his body heat and somehow that thought gave her legs goose bumps. "Am I really that hard on you?"

"Definitely."

"I'm sorry about that. It's just me. I get too sarcastic sometimes I guess."

"It's a defense mechanism."

"Okay, Dr. Phil. So what am I defending against?" Maeve asked.

"Your unbearable attraction to me."

No shit, Sherlock. "Oh really?"

"Sure. I get that from all women."

Maeve laughed at his cocky grin, which suddenly faded.

"Seriously, though, Maeve." His eyes met hers. "What was going on with you tonight?"

"What do you mean?"

"You weren't yourself."

"What are you talking about?"

"You barely looked me in the eye all night. And you got creamed in Scrabble. That's not like you. You're distracted or something."

Maeve pulled her eyes from his, her heart rate quickening. For a split-second, she actually considered telling him the truth—that she had been flustered by having his face so close to hers, feeling that charge of anticipation, believing they would actually kiss. Getting lost in his eyes, the same way she had eight years ago. She had found herself wanting more.

But some truths were better left untold. "I lost my job today," she offered instead.

"What? Oh, Maeve, I'm sorry. Why didn't you say anything at dinner?"

"Lacey and Mick were so happy and excited. I didn't want to ruin the evening. I'll tell them tomorrow, I guess." Maeve stretched her legs in front of her, noticing she was overdue for a pedicure. Another expense that would have to be cut.

"You should have said something. Your friends are here to support you, you know."

His arm draped around her shoulders loosely, nothing more than a friendly gesture, she knew. But tonight, his touch made her melt. Uncomfortable, she didn't know if she should pull away, or succumb to the urge to snuggle closer.

"I'll be fine," she said. "It's my own fault, anyway."

"What do you mean?"

Maeve frowned. "I quit. I found out that I got passed over for that partnership, and I just lost my temper and walked out."

"I don't blame you. You were too good for that place anyway."

"Well, if I had half a brain, I would have bit my tongue till I had another job lined up. It's twice as hard finding a job when you don't have one, you know."

"Why not go into business for yourself?"

"Too risky."

"It's what you've always wanted to do, though."

It bothered her that he knew this. Not once, ever, had she uttered that dream to him, yet he knew—the same way he could effortlessly complete her sentences.

"Right now I just have to find something to pay the bills." She glanced back at her dimly lit house, looking peaceful along the edge of the water. "Or I'll be telling Lacey to list the house."

"Over my dead body. That house is your soul, Maeve."

She smiled, comforted that someone knew how much her home meant to her. "Yeah. My Gram would roll over in her grave. It would be a last resort, believe me. But the money would certainly give me some float till I got a job."

"You're not selling. I won't let that happen. None of us will. You have to stop thinking of yourself as alone in this."

"Could you do me a favor?" Glancing at him, she noticed how his face had been flawlessly sculpted to frame his eyes. She thought how much she'd like to distract herself by begging him to take her right now. With his lovemaking skills—which she remembered so well—she'd be guaranteed to forget about losing her job.

"Name it."

Her eyes met his, and she was lost. Make me forget, she wanted to say. *Take me in your arms and kiss away the image of each pesky bill sitting on my desk.*

She could use a distraction in the form of a man like Jack right now. But the friendship she relied on would disintegrate. And she needed that more.

She pressed her lips together a moment, holding back the words she longed to say, then finally spoke. "Let's just not talk about it right now. Let's just enjoy the stars."

He squeezed her tighter. "You got it. Just remember I'm here for you. We all are."

Shutting her eyes, she let herself rest her head against his shoulder, savoring the sound of the water lapping against the dock and the feel of his strength against her. And almost content in the friendship she shared with him.

Almost.

CHAPTER 2

UNCLASSIFIED//FOR OFFICIAL USE ONLY
This is a By Name Request (BNR) for LT JACK FALCONE, USN, to fill 1A-SOJTF-0037-02 starting no later than 21 JUNE. Report to Development Group Commander upon arrival. Excerpt of tasker as follows:

DEVGRU CDR requires LT FALCONE, an ASW Warfare Expert, to support the SPECIAL OPERATIONS JOINT TASK FORCE – NAVAL SPECIAL WARFARE GROUP ONE, SEAL TEAM TEN, LITTLE CREEK, VA for a period of TWENTY-FOUR (24) MONTHS. USNA will fill the requirement listed below in the tasking summary sheet. USNA will ensure the MBR ...

Jack's eyes drifted as he sat motionless in front of his monitor.

E-mail seemed a damned impersonal way to uproot a person for the next two years. But such was the life in the military.

Little Creek wasn't far from Annapolis. Just a half day's drive if the traffic was good. But he couldn't imagine he'd be ashore long. And being on twenty-four hour alert with the SEALs would mean there wouldn't be many weekend trips to Annapolis or anywhere.

Leaning back in his chair, he glanced out the window. The sun was lower in the sky, casting a yellow glow on the historic buildings that filled the campus of the U.S. Naval Academy. Like a postcard, the dome of the Chapel loomed in the distance, just as it had since 1908.

There was a timeless quality to this place. A snapshot today would strongly resemble the ones he and his parents took when they first toured the Academy fifteen years ago. Even the uniforms had barely changed.

God, he was going to miss this place. His surroundings had calmed him, beckoning him to an earlier, easier time in his life. A time when he didn't wake up in a cold sweat in the middle of the night wondering, "What if?"

What if he wasn't strong enough? Quick enough? What if his hands weren't as deft and his mind wasn't as sharp as they usually were?

What if next time, people died because he wasn't good enough?

Landing this teaching position was something of a reward for his service on his last mission, a favor called in by his former Commanding Officer. But he wasn't ready to leave. Not this time. There were still things that needed to be done in Annapolis, but the Navy wouldn't care that he had unfinished business here. Keeping the nation safe somehow eclipsed Jack's need to have a little more time with Maeve.

Maeve. He shut his eyes, and could almost feel her again, her gentle weight in his arms as her eyes gazed up at him through those thick, long lashes, when he had swept her into his arms. He had only meant it as a joke—the way they always joked about things—and was fully prepared to get smacked by one of those designer bags she was always carrying.

He wasn't expecting the blush that crept up her neck to her cheeks, or her quickened heartbeat. For a woman who had been telling him she wanted nothing more than friendship from him, her knees had certainly turned to Jell-O when he held her in his arms.

What could he do about it now, with only six weeks left in Annapolis?

The creak of the door behind him didn't pull his eyes away from the window. "So, do you know about this?" he asked, tossing his head in the direction of his monitor.

Mick stood behind him and glanced at Jack's open email. "Might have heard something. Pretty flattering actually. You were a by-name request for the job. You impressed the hell out of them on that NATO mission."

"Isn't it like the Navy to reward good work with more work?"

"You're the best man for the job," Mick countered.

"Best man," Jack scoffed. "You mean I'm the *only* man for the job. Most nuclear physics guys would snap in two when they hit the water. They can't keep up with SEALs."

"You had an easy enough time on your last mission. Two SEALs came home alive only because you knew how to handle an HK416 better than any physics nerd I've ever known."

Jack frowned.

Mick sat, stretching his legs in front of him, and glanced at his friend. "You know, they'll be giving you an award for that one."

"What?"

"That stunt you pulled in the Baltic."

A dull throbbing building in his head, Jack pressed his fingers to his temples. He didn't like thinking about it. Thank God the mission had been black ops because if it had ever hit the press, his poor mother would have had a heart attack learning that her only son had just disabled a nuclear submarine while under heavy small arms fire.

He had come to Annapolis to shake the memories. It wasn't the fear of dying that kept him awake. It was the fear of failing.

Mick was different. He glanced at the officemate who had quickly become one of his closest friends these past years. Mick was a SEAL to the core, part of the team. Jack wasn't one of them. As an augmentee, he was called because he was needed by them. There was always something that needed to be done that none of them could do by themselves. There were no teammates who could back him up. No contingency plans.

If Jack had failed his last mission, a group of terrorists would have ended their day in control of a nuclear submarine.

Failure was not an option for Jack Falcone.

Jack leaned back from his computer, crawling out of the memory that he felt himself falling into. An award? Wasn't it reward enough to have just survived? "Yeah, maybe I'll get something in a decade or two, knowing how long the paperwork takes on those things."

"And, uh, if you were to get an award, I'd probably be the one to set up the ceremony."

Jack eyed Mick suspiciously, a quiet curse escaping him. "You know something, don't you?"

Mick shrugged. "If I did, I might be asking you who you'd like to invite."

Resting his forehead on his hand, Jack gripped his head, the ache behind his eyes growing. He hated all the secrecy the Navy employed to surprise officers with awards—never telling them what the award was till they were standing in front of an audience of peers.

He loathed the pomp and circumstance over something that was just part of doing his job. If they were going to dole out an award to him for something that happened so long ago, why not just hand it to him over pizza and a beer?

Sighing heavily, he finally raised his head from his hands. "Can I convince you to make the ceremony as small as possible?"

Mick turned to him with a grin. "Hell no. You know the Chain of Command loves to make a big deal of these things. It inspires the mids."

Jack shook his head, reaching for his iPhone. "In that case, I'm texting you the number of my mom. She'll know what family to invite. And then just keep the civilians to as few as possible.

Lacey, Maeve, Bess. Maybe the guys from the gym. My department. Your call."

"How about a toast to missing Shipmates after? Maybe at O'Toole's?"

"Good idea. Besides, I'll need a drink after. Just keep it casual, okay?"

Mick snorted, obviously hell bent on a ceremony of dress whites. "Family, close friends. Toast after. That's all the input you're allowed, Lieutenant. They don't get to pin many big awards on around here. You know they'll turn it into a circus."

Jack's eyes wandered back to the open email on his monitor. "So, any ideas why the SEALs need a nuke augmentee again? It can't be good."

The question, unanswered, hovered thick and suffocating in the air. Classified information was on a need-to-know basis. Just because Mick had clearance didn't mean he'd have any clue what Team 10 was up to.

"You should be happy. It's a slam dunk for your career. You've never been one to shy away from PCSing."

"It's different this time."

Mick's mouth hitched up in a half grin. "Yeah. And speaking of Maeve, I saw her sitting on the steps in front of Rickover Hall on my way here. Are you two meeting up tonight?"

Jack glanced at his watch. She was early. That was a first. "What's that supposed to mean— speaking of Maeve?"

Mick pushed his chair out and let his feet rest on the desk. "I'm just sayin'—"

"Maeve has nothing to do with why I don't want to leave Annapolis." Jack snatched up his latest addition to the framed family photos on his desk and thrust it in Mick's direction. "I've got a nephew due in two months. I was hoping to actually be around this time."

Covering his mouth, Mick faked a cough uttering "*Bullshit*" from behind his hand.

Jack turned away and clicked the email shut. "Maeve has nothing to do with it," he repeated, his mind wandering back to the moment when he saw her at O'Toole's two years ago.

It had been a hell of a coincidence, learning that Mick's future fiancée was best friends with the woman Jack had lost his heart to the weekend he graduated from the Academy.

He had given her his number, and was too damn full of himself back then to imagine she wouldn't call him.

Yet she hadn't called.

For a guy with a 160 IQ, how could he have been so stupid to let her slip from his radar? Dumber still, to have let her convince him that she just wanted to be friends for the past couple years.

No woman who just wanted to be friends sizzled under his slightest touch. There was something else holding her back. And now he only had six weeks to figure it out.

He pushed his chair back from his desk and gathered his notes for next week's classes. He enjoyed teaching physics—working out the puzzles of the universe with formulas that came so easily to him. But right now, he'd prefer spending time figuring out the puzzle that was Maeve.

Mick turned his chair. "So, are you meeting her, or is she just hanging out there to hit on unsuspecting Sailors?"

"Knowing Maeve, it's a little of both." Jack grinned as he logged off his computer. "We're meeting tonight to start addressing the invitations, but she'll probably have the phone number of a few Lieutenants before I get down there."

"Invitations?"

Jack stood up. "Was wondering if that would fly over your head or not. Yeah, invitations. *Your* invitations. I picked them up at the printer today." He reached for a box on the windowsill.

"How the hell did you get them this quickly?"

"The woman who works at the printer just off the Circle has a thing for Navy guys and put our order in front of the queue."

"I'm not going to ask what you had to do to pull this off, then."

"Nothing. She's about seventy and was married to a Chief Petty Officer who served in the Gulf of Tonkin during Vietnam." Jack watched Mick lightly trace the embossed letters on the card. "Makes it official, doesn't it? Hope you weren't thinking of changing your mind."

"Never." Still eyeing the red lettering, he cocked his head. "But the date's wrong, Jack."

"What?" Jack snatched the card, his blood curdling. How could that have happened? He had proofed it so many times that the printer must have thought he was OCD.

Mick laughed. "Kidding, man. They're perfect."

"You son of a bitch. I'll get you back for that."

"I have no doubt you will." Mick gently placed the invitation back in the box. "Want Lacey and me to drop by tonight after we get done interviewing photographers? We're only meeting with two. Everyone else we called was booked solid for June. Shouldn't be too late."

"Nah. Bess is meeting us at my place at six after her last class. We'll have it done in no time."

Mick affectionately punched Jack on the shoulder. "Thanks again for doing all this. It means a lot to Lacey. And me."

"No problem." Jack grabbed the box and tucked it in a football-hold. "I better get down to Maeve before she leaves with some other guy."

He had six weeks to convince her to be his. It wouldn't help his plan to have her distracted by some other Sailor who marched out of Rickover Hall.

Failure was not an option for Jack Falcone.

A pair of seagulls dove into the water, one emerging with a small fish in its beak, just as a flurry of Midshipmen burst through a set of glass doors headed to another class.

She wasn't used to arriving someplace so early, but had no idea how much faster she could walk in flats till today. May as well take advantage of the time and start surfing the web for a job. Between the backdrop of the Severn and the heavy dose of testosterone that permeated through the air, she couldn't have found a more invigorating place to launch a job search, even though the setting was distracting as hell.

Mids poured out of Nimitz Hall. They were so young—plebes, maybe. Skinny and less confident in their stride than their older classmates. It was amazing the transformation that took place here at the Naval Academy in four years. She wondered what Jack looked like when he first arrived here. Certainly not like the young ensign she had a fling with the weekend of his graduation. And definitely not the man he had become today.

As a breeze rolled over the Severn River, her eyes drifted, followed by her mind. *Jack.* Life was a lot simpler before he had slipped back into her life. The divorce was final. Her scars, both literal and figurative, were as healed as they'd ever be. And her new crop of friends didn't remind her of her past years in hell.

Pursing her lips together, she pulled her eyes from the view and typed in the address of a popular job site. She punched in a few words, checked off a couple boxes, and held her breath as she hit "search."

What she saw was bleak. There weren't many jobs out there for interior designers, even ones willing to commute to Baltimore or DC. If she wanted a regular paycheck, she knew where she'd have to look…

Retail. She could picture herself now, trapped on a showroom floor surrounded by a sea of couches and recliners. It was honest work, and she could still vent a little creativity helping clients go through swatches and working up furniture arrangements on the cookie-cutter software programs that most major stores offered customers these days.

But it wasn't what she wanted. She loved the thrill of walking into someone's house, seeing its potential, transforming it so that when they first saw their big reveal, their faces would light up like little children on Christmas morning.

Sullen, her eyes floated upwards to the view again, her mind wandering to what Jack had said. Build her own business? Not now. Not with bills to pay, one housemate leaving her, and the other one broke.

Looking grim, she shut her laptop and watched quietly as a few officers strolled by, teachers like Jack, presumably. She could always tell the single ones—or at least she hoped they were single—because they would invariably glance her way. She felt bolstered by it. Even in boring flats, she could still turn heads.

Carelessly, she tossed them a smile in return. Maeve knew she hit the genetic lottery when it came to her looks. But inside, she felt like damaged goods—that pretty vase at Macy's that everyone wants on their table till someone sees a tiny chip or hairline crack, and decides it needs to be put on the marked-down shelf for 75% off.

Sure, she could still turn heads. But later they'd always be disappointed she wasn't the "10" they'd presumed she was.

Another officer strolled toward her. She didn't know the first thing about rank insignias, but she could tell he was someone important by how quickly the younger ones snapped to attention and saluted.

Her eyes met his and shared a glimmer of recognition. Recollecting his steely blue eyes as he came closer, Maeve felt the strangest flutter in her stomach. "I remember you," she said. "Mick's old SEAL commander, right?"

His broad smile boasted perfectly aligned, white teeth. Maeve imagined his teeth wouldn't dare *not* be straight. A guy this tough would pull out any misaligned tooth with his bare hands and smash it back into a proper position.

God, SEALs were sexy as hell. No wonder Lacey fell so hard for Mick.

"Old? That's a dagger to the heart," he said. As he held his hands to his chest for dramatic flair, Maeve couldn't resist noticing the muscles in his forearms.

"Sorry. *Former* commander," she corrected.

"Good memory. I saw you at Mick's the day I called him back to the SEALs. You must be his fiancée." He reached down, extending his hand.

Maeve laughed as she shook it. "No. Just his friend. Actually, I'm going to be a bridesmaid in his wedding."

"Wedding? That's news to me and I just talked to him last week. They set a date?"

"It'll be in six weeks. We're sending out invitations today."

"Hope I'm on that list."

Raising her eyebrows, Maeve smiled coyly. "Well, now, I could tell you but you haven't given me your name yet, have you?" A hint of her southern drawl came out. What was it about men like him that brought out her inner belle?

"You're right, Ma'am. Joe Shey. Mind if I share your step?" He gave a slight nod to the empty space alongside her.

She patted the pavement. "Maeve Fischer. And I'd love the company. Are you stationed here now?"

"No. I come up every so often to talk to the mids about BUDS and life in the SEALs."

"So… Joe Shey." Maeve glanced down at her computer and opened an Excel sheet. "Joseph A. Shey, Captain. Yep. You're on the list."

"Good. I can look forward to seeing you there, then. Of course, if I could take you out next time I'm in town, then I wouldn't have to wait so long."

"Love to." Maeve caught a glimpse of Jack bounding down the steps toward them, and a hint of guilt pinched her heart. Why was that? Jack and she were just friends. It wasn't as though he hadn't dated half of Annapolis in the time he had been stationed here.

She waggled her fingers at Jack innocently as he approached, and then turned her attention back to Joe. "Let me give you my number."

Joe glanced over to see Jack approaching. "No need. I'll find you."

As Jack's eyes met Joe's he snapped a salute. "Sir."

Standing, Joe returned the salute. "Falcone, heard you were joining Team 10 this summer."

"Yes, Sir. Just found out today."

"They're a good team with a hell of a CO."

"Yes, Sir."

Joe turned his attention back to Maeve. "Good to see you again, Maeve," he said and strode off.

Maeve's eyes couldn't resist following him down the stairs and across the street. Joe had a magnetic presence that she imagined worked well for him in the Navy. He commanded attention with no effort at all.

Jack's voice was clipped as he offered a hand to Maeve, and eased her off the step. "Do you know him?"

"Joe?" Maeve shrugged carelessly as they walked toward the parking lot. "I ran into him at Mick's house once."

He stopped. "Joe?"

"Yeah. Joe."

Squinting his eyes against the late day sun, Jack looked surly. "He's Captain Shey to the rest of us." Raising an eyebrow, he must have noticed that she hadn't yet pulled her eyes from Joe disappearing into the distance ahead of them. "Isn't he older than you go for?"

"If older men all looked like that, I wouldn't have to date younger men." She smiled, and then let her grin fade. "Why did he say you're going somewhere this summer, anyway? You're not leaving Annapolis till next year."

"I'm slated for an augmentee position with Team 10. Just found out myself, actually. That'll teach me not to get behind in email."

"What's Team 10? Some team of physics experts or something?"

Jack laughed. "No. SEAL Team 10."

Maeve frowned. "But you're not a SEAL."

"Right. But sometimes they need guys with particular experience to augment a mission."

Panic edging into her heart, she froze on the sidewalk. "Why would they want you?"

She hadn't meant it to sound insulting. She just didn't like the idea of Jack on dangerous missions. She'd rather picture him in his cute khakis at the front of a lecture hall, droning on about formulas or some other nonsense.

Safe. That's what guys like Jack were supposed to be. Safe. Didn't he know that?

Jack narrowed his eyes. "My nuclear experience."

"But you're an academic. You're a teacher, right?" Maeve had always thought of Jack as a nerdy brain trapped inside an Oh-My-God-bod that was too damn handsome to be risked doing anything dangerous.

"This Academy post is actually the first time I've ever taught. Most of my time, I'm on nuclear submarines." Resuming a brisk walk toward his truck, he didn't even glance her way as he said, "Do you want to write out the invitations today, or not? Because insulting my career isn't part of the plan this evening."

"I'm sorry. Really." Reaching out for his hand, she felt a connection when they touched, just as she always did. "I'm just shocked. That's all. And worried."

His eyes met hers. "That's the nicest thing you've said to me so far today. Come on. My truck's just over there."

Silently mulling the situation, Maeve followed him. "Why don't you live on base like Mick?"

"I'd rather get the housing allowance and live someplace cheaper. I'm saving for something special." He opened the truck's door for her. "Besides, I don't feel like I've got some senior officers looking over my shoulder all the time this way."

"Okay, I'll bite. What are you saving for?" she asked, climbing into his truck.

Jack grinned, eyes cloaked in mystery. "Maybe you'll get lucky one day and I'll show you."

On the short drive to Jack's, Maeve watched the streetlamps whiz by as they crossed the Naval Academy bridge. They turned onto a neighborhood street lined with puffy cherry trees, and Maeve's eyes wandered to the picket fenced houses they passed. Each one, she would bet, was filled with a family.

Kids. Her eyes drifted to a little boy and girl as they turned another corner. They looked at Jack's approaching truck expectantly, standing behind a homemade lemonade stand and waving hopefully. Jack would stop for them, she knew. He was a sucker for kids. They could charge him $5 a cup, and he'd still be opening his wallet.

Feeling a pinch at her heart, Maeve was almost grateful for the reminder of why a relationship with him would never work.

Jack opened the window to what appeared to be a blonde brother and his freckle-faced red-haired sister. Maeve hoped their parents appreciated the gift they had in their children.

Jack glanced at Maeve and said under his breath, "Hope you like lemonade." He turned to the children. "How's business today?"

The girl spoke up first. "Nothing yet. Do you want some?"

"Do I ever," Jack said with feigned enthusiasm. "I'll take one for myself and one for my friend here." He pulled out his wallet.

Glowing at the sight of crisp bills passing through the window, the little boy shouted over the hum of the motor. "Thanks, Mister Jack!" His slight lisp and crooked smile made him almost as endearing as the Sailor sitting next to her who was always willing to stop for a child's lemonade stand.

Some woman would hit the lottery when she found Jack. Some woman other than her. Maeve bit her lip uneasily at the thought.

"Thank *you*," Jack said. After handing a cup to Maeve, he chugged his quickly. "Just what I needed." Giving a wink, he rolled up the window and continued down the street.

"You know them?"

"Lexi and Grayson. Neighbors," he added as he turned into a driveway leading to a charming waterfront colonial with a view of the Naval Academy in the distance.

Maeve gasped. "You live here?"

"Mmhm."

"Why the hell aren't we having Scrabble nights at your place rather than mine? This place is huge."

Jack laughed. "Because I live in a basement apartment here. A retired Navy couple owns the place. It's small, but the location is perfect. I can launch my kayak right off their shoreline. When

I'm not at your place eating Bess's latest, that's usually what I'm doing."

So that's how you maintain a body like that. Kayaking. As he stepped out of the truck, Maeve gave a stealth glance again at his build, how his thick arms led a path to a broad back corded with muscles. Yep, that made sense, she thought, her mind imagining him rowing a kayak along the Severn, the sweat on his body glistening under the late day sun.

She'd bet half the women of this community were perched at their windows with binoculars every time Jack hit the water.

She stepped out of the truck after he opened her door. "I'm jealous. This view is better than mine."

Slipping alongside her as she walked toward the water, he lazily rested his arm across her shoulders. "Depends what you're looking for. You've got the Bay. They've got the Severn."

He gestured toward stairs leading down to a bright red door. "I'll show you the invitations. Is Bess still coming?"

"I've called her three times to remind her, but she never picks up." Once inside, Maeve's expression twisted in disapproval, understanding now why they weren't hanging out at Jack's as often as they did at her home. Small, and crowded with cardboard boxes, his apartment had serviceable furniture that lacked any style. Not a single splash of color.

God, the place could use an interior designer. Maeve wished she had known earlier. She could have made this place "home" for him, rather than just a place to sleep, eat chili, and clean his uniforms. And now he was going. She felt a lump in her throat.

She ventured to a row of boxes along the wall. "What's all this?" Without even considering herself nosy—only curious, of course—she peeked inside.

Jack sidled up next to her. "Old desert cammies. Gear I was issued, but won't need here. Stuff like that." A hint of a smile edged up his face. "Help yourself, Maeve. Don't want you to feel nosy or something."

She glanced at him. "I'm not nosy. Just curious. What do you have desert cammies for? Thought you said you were on subs most the time."

"When the war broke out, I volunteered for a tour in Afghanistan after my first sub tour. The forces were pretty depleted and tired. Chief of Naval Operations asked the Navy to help fill in where the Army and Marine Corps were short."

She moved onto another box, spotting stacks of papers and files. "Why don't you unpack all this? You've been here almost two years, for Pete's sake."

"Waste of time to unpack the stuff I'm not going to use anyway. It will just get re-packed when I PCS again." He set down the white box he was carrying on the console table.

"PCS?"

"Move. It's what we call a military move. Permanent Change of Station. But there's nothing permanent about it. That's why lots of us just don't even bother unpacking everything."

"But that's terrible. This is your home. You should make it a place that welcomes you each night after work. Next time you get a place, I'm going to decorate it for you. You really need help." Leaning over, she gently flipped through a group of frames leaning against the wall. "You've got good stuff to work with, though. What is all this?"

"Awards, mostly. They give you something framed just about every time you leave a job. Signed photos, plaques, stuff like that."

"You should have all this displayed."

Jack shrugged as he went to a small college-style fridge and grabbed a Sam Adams. "Want something to drink?"

"No. The lemonade was enough. I needed it. Got hot out there waiting for you."

"I was on time."

"Yeah. I was early. Great view to look for jobs online though."

Slumping his broad stature slightly—a rare sight—he said, "I wish you wouldn't do that."

"Do what?"

"Look for a job working for someone else. You have too much talent to not have your own name on the door."

"I need a guaranteed income. I may have inherited my house free-and-clear from Gram, but I still have expenses."

"You've got rental income."

"From Lacey, yeah. But she's leaving in a couple months. And I told Bess to stop paying rent and put it towards tuition."

Cocking his head, Jack raised his eyebrows.

"Don't look at me like that. She's practically family, you know? You'd do the same. It won't be forever. She's got only a few more classes before she graduates. And then she can stop cleaning houses for a living. It's selfish really. I just can't stand her walking into the house reeking of Ajax." She smiled.

Jack pressed his lips together thoughtfully. "Could you charge more for Lacey's room when you find a new renter?"

Maeve sank into the couch, nearly wincing at the sound of pleather rubbing against her cotton skirt. Pleather, and probably a Craig's List acquisition found curbside. God, this man needed help. "I could. But I'm not sure where I'm going to find a renter who I'll trust in the house with Abigail." Having a baby in the house really raised the stakes on security in Maeve's mind.

Jack sat beside her. "I hadn't thought of that." He rubbed his five o'clock shadow. "Look. I have money. Like I told you, I'm a saver. No strings attached, Maeve."

Maeve just stared, lost in his green eyes and hard-to-comprehend earnestness.

"I could help with the start-up costs. Get you a website. Maybe some advertising in that free magazine you see all over Annapolis." Sitting next to her, his hand touched her leg innocently. "It's like you said about Bess. You're like family. I want to help."

She was torn between crying from his sincerity and laughing from the sheer irony of what he had said. *Family?* If Jack was just family, why were her panties growing moist simply from having his hand on her knee?

Oblivious, he scooted closer. "I just don't want to see you waste your talent on the wrong company again. Just think about it, okay?"

"Okay," she murmured, her eyes still locked on his as her skin simmered beneath her cotton top. "And thanks. That really means a lot."

Tossing his hands aside casually as he rose, he walked to his console table and picked up a box. "I've seen your work. I think it's a good investment." He passed it to her. "Now. Ready to be wowed?"

She opened it, and felt a grin spreading across her face. The invitations were classic. Just as she had imagined. Scrolling raised red lettering on textured white stock with a tasteful border. "Couldn't be more perfect."

"That's what all the women say about me. But what do you think of the cards?"

Maeve laughed. "They're not so bad either." She thumbed through the contents. "I can't believe you got them printed so quickly. You're a miracle worker. If we don't give people enough time to make plans to come, then we're sunk." She stared at her best friend's name on the card. "Wow. I guess this is really going to happen, isn't it?"

"Lacey and Mick. It's going to work for them, you know," Jack said, seeming to spot the skepticism building in Maeve's eyes.

"It has to. It just does. She loves him so damn much."

"It will." Jack gave her a friendly squeeze that seemed to last a second longer than it should.

And yet not nearly long enough for Maeve.

"So… invitations. Check. What's next, wedding planner?"

"*Everything*. Bess called six different caterers that got good reviews online and had no luck with any of them. Everyone is booked next month. I still haven't found any kind of arch or arbor for where they'll actually say their vows that doesn't look cheesy or mass-produced."

"Ouch. You've just described half my furniture."

Maeve smirked, and glanced around the room in mock appraisal. "Yeah, I wasn't going to say anything, but now that you mention it—"

"You don't really need an arch. The view itself is great."

"But I need to define the ceremony space." She exhaled slowly, picturing a white arch draped in delicate sheers, punctuated by roses.

"Try a garden store. You know, one of those arches that you grow vines on. My mom has one for her raspberries."

Maeve's shoulders drooped. "That's not the kind I'm picturing. I want something… different." She paused. "Something that has a more surprising profile to it. I don't know…" Her voice trailed as she pulled from her purse the set of calligraphy pens she had bought. She handed him one. "Then there's the dress. I already called a couple bridal boutiques and they literally laughed when I told them I needed a dress in six weeks. There's a few samples we're going to look at, but from the descriptions, I don't think they'll pan out."

"Why not?"

"The designers are too over-the-top for Lacey. Picture bling on steroids."

"Yeah. That won't work for her. Besides, for a backyard wedding, she needs something a bit understated. And nothing with a cathedral train. Maybe an a-line or mermaid."

Maeve's jaw dropped. "How does a man who has a sword and a stack of cammies know so much about wedding gowns? You're freaking me out here."

"I have four sisters, remember? I've had to survive more wedding gown talk than you've probably heard in your life."

Not these days, Maeve pondered. For the past two days she had watched every bridal reality show on TV and set her DVR to record them indefinitely. Styles had changed so much since her ill-fated wedding years ago, and Maeve had some catching up to do.

She sat at the tiny kitchen table he had just cleared off. "So, we're going to try one of those huge bridal warehouse places off the beltway." Maeve couldn't resist a cringe. "Lacey won't mind that she's wearing designer knock-offs and they have most of the dresses in stock."

"She'll look great in whatever she wears. I never understood the big deal about weddings anyway. All the work and money for just one day. Seems like some people want the wedding more than they do the marriage."

"Mine was a nightmare."

Jack emptied the box of invitations, reply cards, and envelopes. "The wedding or the marriage?"

Maeve scoffed. "Both."

"You deserved better."

A vision crept into her head that moment—of Jack eight years earlier getting dressed in his Navy whites after their weekend fling. "Call me, Maeve," he had said as he handed her his number.

She never did.

I had my chance at "better."

Lips pursed together, she couldn't resist touching his hand as it rested on the table alongside her, tempted to take it into her own. The instant of warmth that passed between them from the touch was unmistakable—the same magnetism she always felt—making it agony to pull away.

But pull away she did, and she reached for the first invitation. "So, the list is on my laptop. Ready to get to work?"

CHAPTER 3

Sitting on the back porch, Bess's fingers tapped on the keyboard of her borrowed laptop, before slowing again to appreciate the view. A thick fog hung over the mirror-still Bay making this overcast day eerily stunning.

There was silence—and Bess savored it. From the baby monitor alongside her laptop she could only hear a gentle sigh from Abigail from time to time.

Biting her lip, she looked back down at her computer reminding herself to snap out of it. She had work to do. If it had been any other kind of homework, she'd never attempt to do it on the back porch with the beckoning water as a distraction. But designing a web site for Maeve as a final project for her class was an enjoyable way to round out her semester.

She searched her files for a photo of Maeve that Lacey had taken when they were on the water taxi to Eastport. The photo was perfect for her bio page, with Maeve's gorgeous hair tousled in the wind and the crab pots bobbing in the water behind her.

The camera loved Maeve, and didn't she know it? But looking too perfect might be off-putting to potential female clients. She needed to look approachable. In this picture, she looked like the trusted friend that Bess knew her to be.

She grinned when, after a few clicks, the photo appeared on the page in just the right place under her banner. Building a webpage was a little like creating a tasty new recipe—her preferred way of spending her scarce free time. Take a little of this, throw in a little of that, a pinch of spice in the form of clip art, add some meat in the form of text, and *Voilà*! She had managed to create something beautiful from disparate parts.

Clicking save, her eyes wandered again. Touched by the fog, Maeve's small dock seemed to disappear into the Bay. Bess wished the serenity of the view would somehow soothe her jittery nerves. She wasn't looking forward to having this conversation with Maeve. How would she react? And what if she said no?

Her stomach lurched momentarily at the sound of the front door closing and someone punching in the code to Maeve's security system. She slammed the laptop shut, wanting the website to be a surprise for Maeve. Best to wait till it was complete.

Framed in the door, Maeve rested her hand on her hip. "Where-in-the-Sam-Hill were you last night? You were supposed to help Jack and me address the invitations, remember?"

Bess faked a dawning recollection. "Oh, Maeve. I totally forgot."

"I left three messages on your cell phone."

"You know I keep it off most the time." At least that was not a lie. Bess preferred to save her money and kept a burner phone on her for use only in emergencies. "I hope you weren't worried."

"No. I checked with Lacey and she said you were at school late."

"I'm so sorry."

"Don't worry about it. Jack and I got them done, even though my hand is still cramping up from it. Ninety-two invitations. I just hope some of them can't come. If everyone brings a guest, that's twice the people I'm hoping for."

"Mick swears half of them won't."

"Hope he's right. So, invitations are done. Lacey and Mick picked out a photographer last night. That's two things off our list." She sat beside Bess. "What's your contribution to the wedding planning efforts, lazy bum?"

Bess grinned. "Well, seeing as Abby took her first steps this morning, I'm thinking I can offer one really cute flower girl."

Maeve's eyes filled, exactly as Bess knew they would. "Oh, you're kidding. Our little girl is growing up, isn't she?" She touched her hand to her lips as though to suppress a small sob. For a person who always said she didn't want children, Maeve certainly was emotional about every milestone in Abby's life. "She'll be such a perfect flower girl. We'll have you walk her down the aisle. I don't want her to take a tumble."

"I was thinking both of us could walk her. One of us on each side."

Maeve let a tear fall. She was a predictable sap when it came to Abby. "That would make me so happy."

"Great. Hoping that makes up for my bailing on you and Jack last night."

"Completely. But you better not do it again."

Not using the same excuse she wouldn't. Truth was, Bess was determined to make Maeve and Jack spend as much time alone together as possible. There was no hiding that blush that crept up on Maeve when Jack whisked her into his arms the other night.

Maeve might deny she wanted anything more than friendship with Jack. But Bess knew the truth.

Sitting beside Bess, Maeve glanced at the laptop. "What are you working on?"

"I'm supposed to build a website for a final. It's actually fun, but I just can't concentrate on it anymore."

"Why not?"

Glancing sideways at Maeve, she bit her lip. "I was talking to Tyler this afternoon. He wanted to let me know he sent a belated birthday gift for Abby. He just finished Ranger School, and they don't exactly have shopping and post offices available to them there."

"That was sweet." Maeve grinned. "Tyler. Well, no wonder you're distracted."

A swarm of butterflies was loose in Bess's stomach as the image of Tyler in his Army uniform slipped into her mind. He was the unattainable crush for her ever since she had met him last year while he was a West Point exchange student at the Academy for a semester.

He probably never would have stayed in touch with Bess if he hadn't been the one to drive her to the hospital when she had gone into labor. Every once in a while, she'd email him her latest photo of Abby, and for some unknown reason, he'd reciprocate by sending her baby a gift or two from time to time. He probably was just feeling sorry for the pathetic, single mom that she was. "It's not like that. We're just friends."

"Friends don't make you blush like that," she said, lightly flicking her finger against one of Bess's cheeks.

"You should talk."

"What's that supposed to mean?"

"You were practically on fire a couple nights ago when Jack laid his bad pick-up line on you."

Maeve shifted uncomfortably. "Took me by surprise, that's all. So, um, what's going on with Tyler?"

"Well, he happened to mention that one of the first things they have you do in Ranger School is write a will."

"How depressing. And it got you worried about him."

"Yeah, but it also got me thinking. I don't have one."

"A will? Good point. You know, you can do it online, I think. You don't even need a lawyer. No worries."

"Yeah. That's not what has me worried."

"What is it?"

"Well, think about it. If something happened to me, I wouldn't want Abby going to my parents. We haven't even spoken since I finally told them I had a baby. They've pretty much disowned me till I come back to them groveling—and with a husband in tow."

"Good riddance to them."

"And obviously, I wouldn't want her to go to Dan—not that he'd ever figure out he was the father. But still."

Maeve rested her hand on Bess's shoulder. "None of us would ever let Abby go to that abusive son-of-a-bitch. You don't have to worry about that."

Good, Bess thought. This conversation was headed in the right direction. "So I got thinking about who I'd want to raise her if something ever happened to me. And the first person who came to mind is you."

Maeve eyes flew to hers, stunned.

"I mean, I know you always say you never want kids, but there's just a connection between you and Abby that really is so strong." It was undeniable how much Abigail loved being in Maeve's arms, and at times, Bess even felt a little jealous of the adoration.

Maeve looked uncomfortable. "What about Mick and Lacey? They'll be married and I know they want kids."

Bess's heart sank. "I'm sorry. You're right. And they'd be fine. I know you've said you didn't want kids. I just thought… Well, I don't know. Forget I said anything." Bess started to get up from her chair.

"Wait." Maeve touched her arm. "You've got it wrong. I don't think I've ever been so flattered in my whole life. It's just that—"

"I know. You don't have to say anything. Really."

"No, you don't know. And I guess it's time you did." Maeve sighed as she leaned forward in her chair. "I know I say all the time that I don't want kids. But actually the fact is, I just can't have kids."

"What?"

Maeve took a deep breath. "About five years ago, I was diagnosed with breast cancer."

Bess felt the blood drain from her face. "Oh my God. Maeve."

"I'm okay now. Well, knock wood." She rapped her fist on the wood chair. "But anyway, after three rounds of chemo and two rounds of radiation, the chances are nil that I'll be able to have kids. I was asked if I wanted to meet with a fertility expert and maybe save some eggs before starting treatment, but Alan thought it was a waste of time. At the time, I thought he just wanted me to get treatment quickly—I even thought it was sweet of him to supposedly care more about me than having a baby with me in the future." She tossed a hand in the air. "It's my own fault though. It was my decision. But I was too overwhelmed to even think, much less make a decision like that."

"So there's no chance at all?"

"Not without a miracle. And I think I used up my miracle beating cancer."

"Maeve, I'm so sorry. Why didn't you ever tell me?"

Pushing herself up from the soft back cushion, she moved one of the empty chairs in front of her, and put her feet up. "I don't like telling anybody. Half the reason I moved to Annapolis was to get away from all the worried looks from people. So when I inherited this house and decided to move in, I promised myself that I'd give myself a clean break from it all. As best I can, anyway."

Bess sat silent, suddenly remembering the many shared glances between Lacey and Maeve from time to time. A whispered conversation or two. It had always made her feel like something of an outsider. "Lacey knows." It was a statement, not a question.

Maeve nodded. "Caught me in a weak moment. When you were in the hospital, actually, and we had painted Abby's room. I kind of fell apart on her."

Bess felt guilt pinching her heart, even trying to picture it. Maeve never fell apart. "My God. That must have been hard for you. Watching me pregnant all those months. Welcoming Abigail. Why?"

"Why what?"

"Why would you go through all that for me? You never hinted that it might have been uncomfortable for you." Bess raised her palm to her mouth in a sudden recollection. "God, you even went to the ultrasounds with me. Held my hand when I gave birth."

"Why wouldn't I? You're like my sister, Bess. You and Lacey. You're the closest thing to sisters

I'll ever have, anyway." She laughed. "I love my brother but I don't get to push him around half as much as I do you and Lacey." Maeve rolled her eyes with flourish when Bess let a tear fall. "Oh, don't go getting all emotional on me. Geez, you're almost as bad as Lacey."

Bess laughed, wiping the tear. "Do Jack and Mick know?"

"No." Maeve gave herself a shake. "Not just no. *Hell no.* And I want to keep it that way."

"Why? You need the support of friends."

"I don't. What I need is for people to continue treating me the way they do. What I need is to never look at the pity or worry in someone's eyes again."

Bess nodded slightly. Even though she couldn't agree with Maeve's decision, she'd respect her wishes. "When will you be out of the woods?"

Maeve raised her eyebrows. "When are any of us ever out of the woods when it comes to cancer? Five years cancer-free will a good sign. Ten will be better. But I'm shooting for forever." She paused, glancing at the baby monitor as Abby let out a little gurgle. "So anyway, there's nothing I'd want more than to be your back-up for Abigail if something happened to you. But I think you need to name a back-up for your back-up, you know? Just in case."

Bess stared out at the water, still trying to digest all she had just learned from her friend. "Okay. I'll name you, and then put Lacey and Mick next in line." Bess felt a shudder creeping up her. "God, I don't even like thinking about that."

Maeve grinned. "You dying, or me facing cancer?"

"Neither." She gazed into the grey sky, wishing a beam of light would break through the gloom. "What a crappy friend I am." The words had slipped past her lips, even though she hadn't meant to speak them aloud.

"What are you talking about?"

"I'm so involved in my own life. So focused on Abigail and college. I had no idea you were going through all that."

"Ancient history. Don't feel bad about it. I'm kind of proud that you didn't catch on. I like to keep it to myself."

"But don't you need to talk about things like that? I mean, there are support groups for cancer."

"I guess that works for some people, but it just didn't for me. I went for a couple months and all the women were so much older than me. They all had husbands who had been with them for years—the kind of relationships that can survive something like cancer. And I had... Dickhead." Maeve preferred to not use her ex-husband's name whenever possible. After ditching Maeve after the cancer, he didn't deserve a proper name.

Maeve sighed. "When I moved to Annapolis, I realized it was the perfect chance to escape it all—leave Baltimore and be around people who didn't know about it. I didn't want people feeling sorry for me."

"Is that why you aren't with Jack?"

"What do you mean, 'with Jack'?"

"Come on. We all know there's chemistry there. And this is coming from someone who got a D in Chemistry. You know, a guy like Jack would be nothing but supportive to you for all you've been through."

"I know. But it couldn't go anywhere."

"Why not?" A thought occurring to her, she leaned back in her chair. "Oh—hell. It's because you can't have kids. And Jack wants kids."

"Yeah."

"You could adopt."

Maeve rolled her eyes. "You know, it's always a certainty that someone will bring up adoption within five minutes of meeting someone who can't have kids. It's like it's supposed to be some kind of replacement."

"You can't tell me that you wouldn't love an adopted child just as much as you'd love a biological child. I've seen how much you love Abigail, and she's not yours."

"That's true. And maybe I will one day when I've got a few more years of being cancer-free under my belt. But Jack was bred to breed. And with his brains and bod, it would practically be a sin not to expand his genetic pool." She forced a laugh. "He wants to have his own kids. And I'm not going to live my life feeling guilty that I couldn't give him what he always wanted. Besides, he's kind of a pain in the ass."

"Bullshit."

Maeve tossed back her head in exasperation. "Yeah, he's freaking perfect, isn't he? I'm actually counting down the days till he leaves. I love spending time with him. But it's kind of hard being his friend."

"I can imagine."

"In fact, you owe me big-time for sticking me with him alone yesterday. Would you mind going to the printer with him Thursday night? We were going to make out the wedding programs, but I could kind of use an evening off from him, you know?"

"Sure," Bess offered amicably, gazing back out to the water thoughtfully.

I think I have a migraine scheduled that day.

Hell of a way to spend a Saturday morning.

Locked in an armbar, squirming on the combatives mat, a steady trickle of sweat from Jack's brow dripped into his eye. Futilely, he pulled at Mick's legs to try to spring free until finally unable to take more, he tapped out.

Mick set him free.

Cursing, Jack wiped his brow. "How the hell did I let that happen?"

"You posted your arm on the mat while I had you in the guard. Look, you've got me beat in the ring. When we're boxing, you'll win every time. And your kicks have promise. But if I get you on the ground, you're toast."

"Fights end up on the ground."

"Which is why we're working on it." Mick reached for his duffel and pulled out a bottle of Gatorade. "Had enough?"

"For today."

"We'll work more on the ground next week. That's where you need it." He sat on a bench off to the side of the ring. "You know, you don't have to keep up with the SEALs. They want you for your brain."

"Yeah, but if I didn't know how to take someone down in hand-to-hand combat, that Baltic mission wouldn't have had a happy ending."

"True. I'm just saying don't put too much pressure on yourself."

"You're one to talk." Jack rose, refilling his camelback and swinging it over his shoulder.

"Not hitting the showers?"

"No. I'll take a run home."

"Don't overdo it. You'll be no use to anyone if you're dead. Sit. Hydrate." It was more of an order than a suggestion. His tone suggested he was pulling rank, but Jack knew it was intended more as a pseudo-big-brother than superior officer. "Same time next week?"

"Afternoon would work better. Maeve and I are headed to the Eastern Shore to get some stuff for the wedding. She says she needs my truck. Won't fit in her BMW."

"Likely excuse."

"What do you mean?"

"I think she just wants to spend more time with you. Lacey said she's pretty broken up about you leaving."

"I haven't noticed that."

"Jack, no offense, but you notice nothing less than a nuclear explosion." He swiped a towel across his chest and stood. "And considering your line of work, that's a good thing."

"If anything, I think she's anxious for me to go."

Mick swung open the door to the locker room. "You've got four sisters. You should be able to figure her out."

"This one's beyond me." Jack followed him. "Has Lacey mentioned anything?"

"Hell no. If Maeve confided something, she'd never tell me. The bonds of friendship are stronger than the bonds between future spouses, apparently. Better figure it out fast though, because she's got a date with Captain Shey next week."

Jack's eyes flew to Mick's. "Son of a bitch."

Mick glanced around the locker room. "Better watch that talk about a Captain, Jack."

"What the fuck is he dating Maeve for?"

Cocking his head, Mick raised his eyebrows. "I think you're old enough to figure that out for yourself."

"This doesn't bother you? He's your Commanding Officer, for God's sake."

"*Was* my Commanding Officer. And he's a fifteen-year friend of your new CO in a matter of weeks. So better watch your mouth." Tossing a towel over his shoulders, he started toward the shower. "It's her choice, so don't get stupid about it. It's not like you haven't been in relationships while you've been stationed here. I never heard her gripe about it."

Mick was right. Maeve hadn't shown the slightest jealousy when Lissa's name started coming up regularly in conversations. Or when Lissa was replaced by Krystal. And it bugged the crap out of Jack that she hadn't.

"If you want something with Maeve, it's time to shit or get off the pot," Mick grinned, "as my dear departed grandfather used to say. See ya tomorrow." He disappeared behind the shower curtain.

Jack grumbled his goodbye as he headed out of the gym. He couldn't help the pout that was plastered on his face as he started his run toward the Navy bridge. He ran faster than his usual pace hoping to pound out the jealousy and leave it mashed into the concrete beneath him.

CHAPTER 4

It was a great dream.

She had it often enough this past year that her body should have stopped reacting with a low, sizzling thrum, as though she had just had the best sex imaginable. Yet his image was so clear, so vivid that she'd swear right now she could smell his aftershave mixed with the aromatic steam from a cup of freshly brewed coffee tickling the bottom of her nose.

Coffee? Maeve's eyes flew open to the sight of Jack at her bedside, holding a cup of joe under her nose.

"Jack!" Instinctively, she gave him a shove, sending a splash from the mug flying across her duvet and onto him. "What the hell are you doing in here?"

"Hey—that's hot, Maeve." Jack ripped off his soaked t-shirt, sending Maeve's temperature up ten degrees.

The coffee's not the only thing hot in this room. Maeve tried to pull her eyes from his chiseled six-*no*-eight-pack, but failed miserably. Even in the low light that seeped into the bedroom from the hallway, his abs blazed a magnificent path across his abdomen that seemed to scream, "Touch me, and see if I'm for real!"

Even the simple act of wadding up his shirt to sop up the coffee from her duvet made his forearm muscles bulge in a subtle way that made Maeve's temperature soar. He looked at her. "Is this always how you greet men who bring you breakfast in bed?"

Maeve glanced around. "I don't see any breakfast."

"I brought you coffee. Assumed with that body, you were the skip-breakfast kind of girl." The edges of his mouth crept into a half-smile.

"Shows what you know. And speaking of my body, what are you doing in my room with me half-naked?"

"What's a little skin between friends?" he chided, toying with the sheet she held firmly to her chest.

Sighing, Maeve reached for the lamp. "Seriously, Jack. What are you doing here?"

His face was dead-panned. "You really forgot? We're headed to the Eastern Shore today."

Maeve felt her body sink back into the bed in protest. Why had she agreed to leave so early in the morning just to miss weekend traffic? In the low light she gazed at Jack, who looked as awake at five a.m. as he did at high noon. He had probably already gone for a six-mile run and had breakfast by now. "Okay, okay. I'll be downstairs in two minutes. Now, get out." She tossed a pillow at him as he backed out of the room. "And I could use another cup of coffee."

"What's the magic word?"

"*Now.*"

Jack grinned and slinked out the door.

Hearing the door click shut, Maeve dropped her sheet from her chest. Too close. It's bad enough to be having sex dreams about a friend, but much worse if he wakes her up in the middle of it.

She hadn't thought planning a wedding with Jack would be this difficult. Jack had always been underfoot these past months. On her back porch playing Scrabble. Grilling steaks in her backyard. Hell, he even knew what day was trash day and never failed to take the cans to the curb without even being asked.

Spending a little extra time with him shouldn't have this effect on her.

But alone, Jack was different. Jack was tempting. Every time he touched her, she wanted more. Every time he looked at her, she was entranced. And every time he left, she felt an emptiness that was new to her. She'd just have to resist. He was leaving in four weeks anyway. Surely she could manage that.

But if he took off his shirt again, all bets were off.

Slipping on yoga pants and a t-shirt, she restrained herself from putting on makeup. Being from the South, it should seem a sin, but she'd lived with Yankees long enough not to care.

The stairs creaked beneath her feet, and Maeve cringed, hoping she would not wake the baby. She glanced over to Abby's room and saw Jack peering in, still as a statue, a travel mug of coffee in his hand. Hearing her approach, he passed her the mug and whispered, "She's so cute when she's sleeping."

Maeve warmed, as she always did when looking at her goddaughter. But from her mouth came steely words. "Yeah, but then she wakes up. Crying, usually. If you wake her, we'll be hitting traffic," Maeve warned.

"Worth the risk." He reached in and cradled her in his strong arms, the perfect contrast of virile strength against complete vulnerability. "I haven't seen her all week. She's at least an inch bigger."

Maeve softened as she watched him with her. His exterior was so rugged and tough. Not the least bit of softness in his hard muscular flesh. But inside, he was soft. "A hard-boiled marshmallow," just like Maeve's grandmother used to call her. Gazing at him in the low light, Maeve felt a tug on her heart.

"Come on, Jack." Her harsh whisper broke the sweetness of the moment. "Let's go."

"You're right." He gently placed Abigail back into her crib. "I just can't help myself with that kid."

Stepping out into the chill, Jack walked briskly ahead, and opened the truck's door for her. His mouth edged upward.

"What?" she asked warily.

"I don't think I've ever seen you without makeup in the daylight."

"Technically, it's not really daylight yet." She touched her face unconsciously. "That bad?"

"Actually you look better this way."

Maeve snorted.

He started the truck. "So, what's on the agenda today?

"We'll head to the outlets first. Mostly for table dressing stuff. For the centerpieces, I'm thinking candles in hurricanes if I can find some. Then I'll take rose petals and sprinkle them around the hurricanes for a little extra color. The space is just too small for anything more dramatic on the tables. And there will be plenty of flowers elsewhere."

She popped the lid on her travel mug and took a sip. "Mmm. Perfect. How did you remember I put brown sugar in my coffee?"

At a stoplight now, he turned to her. "I remember everything." The words seemed filled with meaning as his shamrock green eyes seemed to peer straight into her soul. But when the light changed, the moment shattered and Maeve wondered if she had even imagined the connection. "So why did you need my truck for this?"

"I also found a place that has an arbor."

"For rent?"

"Umm. No. To buy. But it's gorgeous, Jack. And I've always wanted an arbor for right in front of the dock."

"Always, huh? Never mentioned it to me."

"Well, I have. It'll be my last big splurge for my house before I go on my unemployed budget. It's not that expensive. We just have to put it together and stain it."

Jack shot her a look. "Put it together?"

"Yeah. All the pieces are cut and sanded. It's made by some carpenter in Easton. It comes with plans. The guy says it's easier than putting together an IKEA desk."

"With everything else we have to do? No wonder you wouldn't tell me what we were getting today."

"It'll be a breeze. We'll do it some Thursday night when it's not raining instead of wasting time playing Scrabble."

"You're just doing this because I'm finally starting to beat you."

"Dream on." She took a sip of her coffee. "I'm thinking a natural stain—like a warm honey tone. Something that will last. Maybe their kids will get married under it one day."

"You're a romantic. Who'd have thought a girl like you has a romantic side?"

"A girl like me?"

Jack pitched his voice up an octave, doing his best Maeve imitation. "'Men are like pets. Sure, they're cute and fun to play with, but cleaning up after them gets old quick.'"

"Did I really say that?" Maeve smiled, impressed with herself. "That's good enough for the inside of a fortune cookie."

Jack laughed. "Okay. I'll haul myself out there to get it on one condition."

"What's that?"

"You let me buy it. You shouldn't be splurging on anything right now."

"I'm not letting you buy me something like that."

Jack flicked on his turn signal as though headed for the next exit. "Guess we're not going then."

"Okay, okay," Maeve quickly said. "That's practically blackmail."

"A man's gotta do, what a man's gotta do. Besides, I spend enough time at your house. I'd like to think I got you something to remember me by when I'm gone."

Maeve stomach clenched. "I don't like thinking of that."

"So let's not."

Maeve's mind wandered, still 200 miles away in a place she'd never been before. Little Creek. What would his life be like there? She glanced out the window to the passing car dealers that pocked this stretch of Highway 50. "Okay, you can buy it. But I'm paying you back as soon as I get a job."

"Yeah, sure."

"I mean it, Jack," she said firmly.

"I know you mean it."

Maeve tensed as Jack slowed past the toll that led to the bridge. "Did you find a place to rent tables?"

"Yeah, that was easy. I talked to some staff at the Officer's Club and they found me a place that will rent us tables, chairs—even plates and silverware. I had no idea you could rent that stuff. I found a company that can bartend, too."

"Oh, that's a relief." As they drove over the massive span of the Bay Bridge, Maeve held her breath as she peered over the side. Gripping the armrest tightly, she hoped Jack didn't notice the whites of her knuckles. In the low morning light, she could see a few boats sprinkled in the water, so tiny beneath them. She hated this bridge. Even after driving over it dozens of times, she still felt the sharp tug of vertigo pulling her eyes to the water below, awaiting a brisk wind that could send them soaring over the side and crashing into the Bay.

"Don't like bridges?"

Damn. The man noticed everything. It always made her feel exposed in his presence. "Just the big ones."

He touched her leg gently. "I'm sorry."

"That's nice, Jack. But both hands on the steering wheel, please. You're freaking me out here."

Going to the Eastern Shore was something one did for a weekend getaway, or to begin the ritualistic Friday migration to Ocean City in the summer that regularly trapped Annapolitans like herself in a clog of traffic.

But now with the Bay Bridge behind her, the drive felt different for Maeve—spontaneous and somehow freeing. The sky was bigger out here, the air fresher, and the water wider.

"How about we catch breakfast?" Jack asked. "I'm not worried about traffic now that we've got the bridge behind us. And we've got some time to kill before the stores open."

Breakfast was innocent enough. Surely she could get through an omelet without picturing him naked. "Okay."

Exiting the highway, Jack stole a quick glance at Maeve. "You okay?"

Maeve didn't dare look into his eyes. She wondered how he could always sense her feelings. It unnerved her, at the same time it comforted her. At the same time it turned her temperature up to broil. "I'm fine."

"No, you're not. What is it? You seem really—distracted." He paused as he pulled into the parking lot of a nondescript diner and turned off the truck.

"Distracted? I'm not distracted."

Maeve tensed, when his hand gently touched her chin, guiding her eyes to meet his. She could swear he was suppressing a smile, as though he knew what his light touch did to her and only meant to antagonize her.

"You're hiding something. I know you too well, Maeve."

"Hiding something? I am not. I'm an open book."

"Ha. Far from it."

"Why? What do you think I'm hiding?"

His eyes full of challenge, he unfastened his seat belt. "This." He leaned toward her so close she could smell the cherry Gatorade on his breath and feel the warmth emanating from behind his crisp polo shirt. He brushed her cheek gently and she froze, speechless, breath quickening. His hand entwined in her hair, and, finding the nape of her neck, he pulled her face closer—so close she could see tiny blue flecks in the sea of green within his eyes. Helpless, she caught herself wetting her lips instinctively, waiting to feel his mouth against hers.

He was going to kiss her. Finally. And she'd let him. Gladly.

"This—" His eyes wandered across her face, taking in every feature, fingers lightly tracing a path from her forehead to her cheeks, her chin, and then resting his finger on her moist lips. "—is what you're hiding. You want to kiss me. Don't deny it."

He paused, and she could only manage a whimper in reply.

"So what's holding you back, Maeve?" Abruptly, he pulled away from her, leaving every cell in her body to ache. "That's what you're hiding."

Having made his point, his eyes were smug, and he unlocked the doors.

Damn him.

Every pore in Maeve's body seemed to sizzle with perspiration. Inhaling deeply, she struggled to resume her composure as he extended his hand to help her out of the truck. She didn't take it. "I don't know what you're talking about."

He gripped her forearm lightly, and placed his thumb on her wrist as he watched the seconds fly by on his watch. "Your pulse is about 140. You can't deny you felt something just now."

She ripped her arm from him, and leaned against the truck. "Don't be an ass. You were just freaking me out coming on to me like that. That's all."

"Bullshit."

Frustrated, she charged toward the diner, as he followed in long, lazy strides behind her. "We're just better as—"

"—friends." Jack finished her sentence for her, the way he so often did. Nonchalant, he opened the door for her. "Works for me."

Works for him. Three words that cut like a knife. Couldn't he at least put up a bit of a fight?

Just friends wasn't working for her. Out of the corner of her eye, she watched him as they waited for the hostess to seat them. He didn't look annoyed. He didn't look frustrated. Hell, he didn't even look aroused—and meanwhile every square inch of her skin longed to cling to him like Saran Wrap.

Comforted by the aroma of strong coffee and sizzling eggs, Maeve slid into a booth just as a flock of seagulls lifted themselves from the bay outside their window.

"Coffee?" he asked her when the waitress arrived, as though the last five minutes had never even happened.

"Yes." She was determined to sound as nonchalant as he did. "Idiot," she muttered under her breath.

Jack burst out laughing, and Maeve couldn't help cracking a smile in return. Trying to distract herself, she looked out the window.

"You're not really mad at me, are you? I'm just calling it like I see it."

"No." Maeve pouted. It was so hard staying angry at Jack, she thought, as he poured creamer in her coffee and asked the waitress for a side of brown sugar. "But for the record, my pulse was up because of the coffee I drank in the car."

"Of course. I should have known that." He nodded sagely, clearly suppressing the grin that was peeking out from the corner of his mouth.

The diner overlooked the east side of Prospect Bay and even through the glass of the window, she could hear a cacophony of morning birdsong outside. Hell of a view for a place that served a $4 omelet. You can't get this on the other side of the Bay Bridge, she thought, trying to focus on the menu. "How did you know about this place? Have you been here before?"

"Back in my senior year at the Academy, a lot of us used to stop here for breakfast on our way to Ocean City. The place has been open forever. My dad used to take us here when he was stationed here, too."

"Your dad? He's in the military?"

"Was, yep. A Marine."

"I didn't know that."

"I'm full of surprises."

Yeah, no kidding. Maeve's mind drifted momentarily to the feel of his breath on her lips, held so close to him. She glanced back down to the menu, unable to meet his eyes. *Focus. Focus.* "Is that why you joined?"

"Maybe a little. My dad never pushed me, but you know, the culture just becomes a part of you growing up. With my grades and SAT scores, I could have gotten in just about anywhere. But the Academy felt like home." Jack pointed to a photo on her menu. "Try the crab stuffed omelet. It's the best."

Maeve's mouth watered at the suggestion.

As Jack ordered for both of them, movement outside the window again drew her eye. Two herons soared past, slicing through the rosy mist that hung over the bay. A group of fishermen walked along the docks together, and a smattering of crabbers bobbed in the water checking on their traps.

Maeve glanced around at the people surrounding her. Not a hint of make-up, not a single stiletto, and no sight of designer handbags. And each person looked perfectly content, satisfied to simply be enjoying a good cup of coffee with their neighbors. While Annapolis was a quaint and laid-back city, it seemed uptight by the Eastern Shore's standards.

She could get used to it here.

"Did you tell your parents you're leaving yet?" Her throat pinched at the thought, and she poured more creamer into her coffee to distract herself.

Jack nodded. "It'll be harder to say good-bye than usual. I've been able to spend so many weekends and holidays visiting them and my sisters. I've gotten kind of used to it. One's got a baby due in July. Did I tell you that already?"

Smiling, Maeve nodded. Several times, actually, she thought. But she didn't tell him that. It was cute to see him so excited about having another nephew coming his way.

"I really hoped I'd be around for the birth this time." His eyes were distant, as though he was counting how many significant moments of his family's lives he had missed while away.

She reached for his hand, and again was struck by how complete she felt when her clasp had joined with his. "I'm sorry."

Frowning, Jack withdrew his hand. "No big deal. You get used to it."

Liar.

"At least I'll be around for Mick's wedding. I haven't been best man for years. Am I still supposed to drag him out to a strip bar and get him drunk the night before?"

"I think that's optional. But Lacey would prefer you didn't."

"So would Mick. He's all control. It's hard enough getting him to have two beers."

"You're pretty controlled yourself."

He eyed her a moment and then gently touched his finger to her chin. "With you, I have to be, don't I? How's the job search going?" He changed the subject without missing a beat.

Maeve traced her thumb along the rim of her mug. "Pretty scary, actually. I called just about everyone I know in the business and no one is hiring. They're all just struggling to find clients right now. But at least I put the word out."

"Well, I had an idea." Jack lifted his hand as Maeve opened her mouth. "And don't shut me down till you've heard it all, okay?"

"Okay," Maeve replied tentatively.

"You know how you said my decorating skills were hopeless?"

"I didn't mean anything insulting about it, though."

"No, no. I didn't take it that way. We Navy guys just don't have any practice on how to settle in and make a place look nice. We move too much. And families have it even worse sometimes because they're trying to do it all while juggling kids." He took a sip of his orange juice. "So how would you feel about offering your design services for free to a few Navy people? You can sort of dress up their places with the stuff they have, maybe a few items they can afford to buy, too, on a tight budget. We take some pictures of it all and then you can write about it on your blog."

"I don't have a blog."

"You need a blog. And it will have a special tab just for your Navy makeovers. We'll call that section something catchy like 'Dress my PCS' or something like that. You know—like a take-off of all those 'Dress-My-This-And-That' shows."

Maeve couldn't suppress a laugh. "Dress my PCS? That's actually funny. You're pretty creative for someone who aced nuclear physics."

"Actually Bess came up with it. We've been— spending some time together."

Spending some time together? What was that supposed to mean? Maeve edged out the childish jealousy that seemed to creep into her stomach. She tried to sound unaffected. "But most people don't even know what a PCS is."

"Details, details. We'll think of something better then." He chugged the last of his orange juice. "You help out Navy people like that and you'll get publicity. I guarantee it. You live in a Navy town. Word will get out and one of these local magazines will want to write an article about you. And the blog will link to your website."

"I don't have a website."

Jack reached for the pepper. "You will by the end of the day."

"*What?*"

He shrugged. "Bess and I have been working on something together. One of her clients is a graphic designer who whipped up a logo for you in exchange for some free housecleaning from Bess. Bess is finishing the website today."

While the cat's away... Maeve struggled not to burst into protest. "Jack, I'm really not comfortable with this."

Jack held up his hands. "We won't publish it till we get your approval, of course. But we just wanted to show you what was possible."

Maeve didn't know whether to kiss him or shake him senseless. Her eyes drifted to his lips and she realized which she'd prefer. She swallowed and leaned her chin on her hand. "I wish you guys wouldn't have done that. I really don't think I have it in me to be self-employed. I'm too—I don't know."

"Risk adverse?"

"Well, yeah."

"How about this? You just try it out a little while you're still looking for a regular job. It's not like you have an offer yet, right?"

"Don't remind me."

"So it's not like you're wasting time. Keep sending out your résumé, and if a job offer comes, great. But in the meantime, there's nothing wrong with passing out a few business cards of your own company."

My own company. "I don't have business cards."

Jack reached into his pocket. "Actually, you do." He plunked a card down in front of her.

Her hands nearly were numb as she lifted it. Maeve Fischer Designs, it read, with her contact information beneath. It was simple and clean with a sleek graphic above her name that looked reminiscent of waves on the Bay. She traced her finger over the raised print and the shiny spot gloss over the logo.

"Do you like it?"

Maeve just stared, speechless.

Jack put his fork down. "Crap. You don't like it?"

Almost embarrassed to see goose bumps popping out on her arms, Maeve blinked several times. "I love it."

Noticeably relieved, Jack lifted his fork and took another bite of his omelet. "Thank God. Because I've got 499 more at home. So will you give it a try?"

"Why are you doing all this for me, Jack?"

Eyes locked on hers, Jack remained silent for a few beats, and then shook his head. "You're always the one doing things for all of us. Hell, I'm at your place as much as I am mine. But it goes both ways, Maeve. You need to let us do things to help you, too."

It should be so easy. But if she accepted his kindness, she felt her heart would get lost to him forever.

Thoughtfully, she looked out the window as the sun's reflection laid out an impressive tangerine carpet along the water. Daybreak was so beautiful, and she rarely had time to enjoy it, stuck in traffic on the way to work every morning.

For a brief moment, she allowed herself to imagine beginning her work day at home, sipping her coffee on the back deck with her laptop in front of her, watching the sunrise. Oh, she could get creative in an atmosphere like that. "Okay," she murmured, almost afraid to say the word aloud.

Jack almost looked shocked. "You'll try it?"

Maeve smiled. "I'll try it." She looked at Jack, and dared to touch her hand to his cheek. The subtle heat from his skin penetrated her, not in the fiery way to which she was accustomed, but with a comforting warmth that seemed to strengthen her. "And thanks, Jack."

He took her hand in his and lightly kissed the underside of her palm, and then quickly set her hand down on the cold table.

CHAPTER 5

Maeve reverently touched the massive box that lay safe in the top of her walk-in closet.

Lacey peered past her. "What is it?"

After carefully pulling it from the shelf, she set it down on her bed and lifted the top. A smile touched her lips at the sight of delicate Irish lace, perfectly preserved, still a rich, clean cream barely showing signs of age.

Lacey drew in a breath. "Is that your grandmother's gown?"

"Mmhm."

"Oh, Maeve, it's beautiful."

"They just don't make gowns like this anymore," Maeve agreed, holding it up to her friend.

"I'm almost afraid to touch it."

"It's in great shape. It won't rip." She guided her friend to the full-length mirror on the back of her bedroom door.

Lacey stared into the mirror. "I love it."

"It's a little old-fashioned. But it would work, especially if we take down the neckline. It's simple and classic—perfect for a backyard wedding. You can wear it, if you want."

"I couldn't."

"Sure you could. Do you know how happy that would have made Gram?" She moved to stand along Lacey, gazing at her friend's radiant reflection. What a beautiful bride, Maeve thought, and imagined Lacey taking Mick's hand at the front of a long carpet blanketed with rose petals, framed by an arbor dripping in flowers.

Letting Lacey borrow Gram's dress hadn't been part of the plan. But after shopping with Lacey for wedding gowns unsuccessfully three times, Maeve was getting a little desperate.

Her eyes still fastened on her own image, Lacey looked wistful. "I'll bet you looked beautiful in this dress, Maeve."

"I did—when I was nine years old and playing dress up," Maeve laughed.

"You didn't wear this when you got married?"

Maeve sat on the bed. "No. I wanted to. But my mom wanted a big Southern nightmare of a wedding. I had to wear this huge dress and a birdcage veil. I even had a parasol, though I refused to use it except in the pictures. I looked like I was in a Civil War reenactment."

Lacey turned. "Maeve, I shouldn't be the one to wear this gown. You should. Geez, it looks like it was made for you. You probably wouldn't even have to take it in."

Maeve actually snorted. "I'm not getting married again. Believe me."

"You don't know that."

"I do."

"Why not?"

"Been there. Done that. Got the t-shirt." Maeve sighed at the sight of Lacey's disbelief, and sank backwards onto her pillows. "Besides, the men I date aren't looking to settle down with someone like me."

Lacey smirked. "Maybe you should stop dating younger men."

"That's harsh."

"I'm serious though. Try dating someone who is on the same page as you are." Lacey shared a conspiratorial grin with her friend. "Still going on that date with Captain Shey?"

Maeve smiled coyly. "How many girls get to go on a date with a SEAL CO? 'Course I'm still going."

"Mick nearly burst an artery when I told him. You, dating his CO."

"Former CO. It's just dinner. It probably won't turn into anything else."

"Does Jack know?"

"Why would I tell him?"

Lacey shrugged, and took another look at herself in the mirror. "This is gorgeous, Maeve."

"So wear it. Nothing would make me happier." She rose and took her friend's hand as they gazed at the dress in the mirror. "Gram had a timeless style about her, didn't she? So? What do you think?"

"I think," she began, stopping to carefully hand Maeve the dress, "that you are the best friend I could ever ask for. But everything in me says that this dress is meant to be worn by you next."

"Lacey—"

"First your grandma, then you. I'm not convinced you won't have a second chance at marriage, Maeve."

Puffing out her cheeks, Maeve let out a breath. "Okay then. Guess we're stuck going shopping again. But you better actually buy something this time. The clock's ticking." Frowning, she put the dress back in the box. If Lacey had her way, she'd get married in jeans and her flip-flops.

There was a light tap on the open door.

"Bess, I didn't know you were home already."

"I left early. Remind me to never go to one of those community playgroups again."

"Oh, no," Lacey said. "Did Abby not get along with the other kids?"

"More like I didn't get along with the other mothers." Bess flopped onto the bed with a stack of the day's mail on her lap. "Oh, they were like vultures and I was the prey. First, one catches wind that Abby hasn't said her first word yet. And she's like, 'Oh, aren't you worried? She should be saying something by now. My baby was saying three word sentences by that age.'"

Maeve's lip curled. "Ugh. The mom-competition begins. That's just the beginning, I hear. Next she'll tell you that her precious child is learning quantum physics and reciting Shakespeare."

"And the doctor told you not to worry about it yet. So don't worry about it," Lacey reminded her.

"Yeah, and I told her that. But then she's got about six other moms in on the conversation, and together they had Abby diagnosed with at least six different things. My blood pressure's never been so high in my life." Bess threw her head back into the pillows. "And then they asked about my husband, so I had to tell them I'm single." Her laugh was almost maniacal. "And then, the shining climax was when they asked me what I did for a living."

Maeve sat beside her, knowing what was coming. "And you told them you clean houses."

Bess nodded. "Next time I'll just lie, because honestly, my half of the room cleared out like I had the plague."

"Bitches."

"Every last one of them." Bess paused. "Except one seemed nice. I didn't talk to her much, but Abby seemed to like playing with her baby boy. We talked a little, and she actually gave me her number so we can get the kids together again. She didn't seem repulsed by the scarlet A embroidered on my chest."

Maeve laughed. "So it sounds worth it."

"I guess, yeah. It sure wore Abby out, too. She was out like a light the moment I set her down in the crib." Bess held up three cards, one with an open envelope. "Oh. And these came in the mail today."

"What are those?"

"Mine's an invitation, so I'm guessing yours are, too. Some kind of award ceremony for Jack. Did you guys know anything about this?"

Lacey eagerly snatched hers from Bess, and ripped open the envelope. "Mick mentioned it to me." She glanced down at the card. "Cool."

Curious, Maeve opened hers. "What's he getting an award for?"

Lacey shrugged. "I asked Mick and he said if he told me, he'd have to kill me."

"Always a nice answer from your fiancé."

"Seriously though, all I know is that he saved a couple guys on his last mission. Mick told me it was something for NATO. That's why he got picked for this next job."

Bess looked quizzical. "All this time, I thought he was a teacher."

Maeve frowned. "Didn't we all? Seems our egghead is leading a second life."

Bess sat up on the bed with a girlish giggle. "Well, with a bod like that, I should have guessed. So, we're all going?"

"Of course. Mick says this is huge. Most of the brigade will be in attendance. A four-star is presenting it to him."

Bess groaned. "Aw, man. Do I have to buy a dress?"

Lacey shook her head. "Nothing special. Just wear something you have."

"What I *have* are five sets of sweats."

Maeve moved to her closet. "What you *have* is half my net worth in clothing to choose from. Better use it now before I have to sell it all on eBay to pay the electric bill."

Bess cocked her head at Maeve. "I'm hardly your size. I'll never fit in anything of yours."

Maeve dug deeper into her closet and pulled out a dress. "Honey, I've been every size in the book." Just looking at the sundress reminded her of cancer treatment. The weight loss, the weight gain. The weight loss again. No wonder she was so damn tired.

Bess's eyes lit. "Ohh, that's pretty, Maeve."

"A few years old, but it still is nice enough, isn't it? I'm glad I never throw anything away. Try it on and see if it fits." She tossed it to her as Bess peeled off her clothes.

"I have earrings that match it." She opened up her jewelry box, and received the usual appreciative "ooooh" from her housemates, as though opening the elegant wooden box was a magical experience. Between the pieces that had been passed down from her grandmother and her own lavish taste in gems, the contents of Maeve's jewelry box were impressive.

Lacey stepped over. "I love it when you start handing out jewelry. Can I borrow something, too?"

"Of course." She dug inside the box, and pulled out a simple chain of gold with a sapphire charm, surrounded by tiny diamonds. "How about this necklace with that blue dress you have? Bet that would be appropriate for an awards ceremony."

"Or maybe—" Looking like a kid in a candy store, Lacey dared to venture into the box herself. "Hey what's this?" She pulled out a Navy medal. "Was this your grandfather's?"

Maeve shook her head. "No. He wasn't in the armed forces. I never saw it till after Gram died, so I never could ask her. But I could picture her falling in love with some Navy officer when she was young. She lived in Pensacola for a while, before she met Grandpa."

Bess reached for the ribboned insignia. "National Defense Service Medal," she read. "Maybe she lost him in the war. She must have really loved him to keep it, even though she married your grandfather."

"War sucks," Lacey said, the statement stronger now that she was marrying someone in the military. "That's so sad."

"It is," Maeve agreed, even though the thought of Gram ever loving a man other than her grandfather somehow unsettled her. She glanced at it, still in Bess's hand. Some loves weren't meant to be, she supposed. "But if it had worked out for them, I wouldn't be here." Sighing, she reached back into her jewelry box. "Oh, hey. How about this, Lacey? It goes with that yellow dress." She handed Lacey a necklace and gestured to her closet.

Bess spied a silk dress in Maeve's closet that still had the tags. "Ooh. Nice." She fingered the imported silk. "When did you get this?"

"Right before I quit. Borrow anything you like, but not that. I'm returning it next time I get into Baltimore."

Lacey pulled out a yellow sheath and held it up to herself. "I like this. So sunny looking." She glanced at Maeve. "What am I going to do living 2700 miles away from you guys?"

Maeve scoffed, "Well, you'll have to go shopping, for one thing."

"I'm serious. And what about when he deploys?" Lacey's eyes welled up.

Maeve gave her a squeeze. "You'll hop on a plane in the morning and be here in time to help Bess make dinner."

Edging up to the other side of Lacey, Bess rested her arm on her shoulders. "Maeve's right. It takes longer to fix a shoulder roast in a slow cooker than it does to fly back here. So if you get lonely, that's what you do."

Maeve darted a look to Bess. "Speaking of food, have you found a caterer yet?"

"Not one. Everyone is booked up in June." Stretching out on the bed again, Bess sulked. "I even called a chain down by the mall just to see if they could do it –you know, that barbeque place?"

"We are *not* serving barbeque at a wedding. Lacey will have sauce all over her dress. I can picture everyone hugging her with sticky fingers."

"Well, you don't have to worry about it because even they are booked. We might have a better chance if we changed the wedding to a Sunday."

"But we already sent out invitations."

"Right." Bess rolled over and propped her head up on her forearms. "I found one place. Can't find any reviews online for them. But I called three of their references, and they checked out." She shrugged. "Who knows though? I might have been calling their friends and family. I'd feel better if they had catered for someone I knew."

"What kind of food?"

"Run of the mill. Chicken, fish, the usual wedding fare."

Maeve frowned. "Doesn't sound too promising."

Lacey gave a light wave of her hands. "They sound good enough."

"Coming from someone who wanted a City Hall wedding, that's not saying much."

Lacey smiled. "If I have Mick there, and you guys and my sister, that's all I need. The rest is icing on the cake."

"Cake!" Bess suddenly bolted upward. "Is anyone checking into a cake yet?"

Maeve stomach lurched. Less than four weeks to go. No dress. No caterer. No cake.

This was going to be one hell of a wedding.

CHAPTER 6

Staring at a closed dressing room door, Maeve talked into her iPhone. "She's got three more she's trying on, Vi. You want me to Skype you in again so you can see?"

From the other end of the phone, Vi's exasperation was palpable. "Do they look any different from the other eight I saw?"

"Not really."

"Then forget it. I have a meeting in five anyway." As one of CNN's most recognizable financial reporters, Lacey's sister had to be efficient with her time. "Just email me a picture if she actually buys something."

"I will. Bess and I were thinking about picking out bridesmaid dresses today. Any objections?" Maeve asked, thinking Vi really should be part of the decision since she was maid of honor.

"Are you kidding? Go ahead and pick out whatever you want. In fact, if you pick something out for me, I'll buy you a case of your favorite Merlot. I'll never get around to it. Have you thought about a bachelorette party?"

"I ran it by Lacey and she doesn't want anything much. She wants to be in bed by 10 so she'll look radiant the next day."

"Probably smart. She's such a lightweight with alcohol. Hold on." Vi started talking to someone else in her office.

Maeve could somehow picture Vi in her designer suit, tapping away at her computer, juggling three or four different conversations at once, all within six inches of a steaming cup of Starbucks.

"Sorry about that," Vi said into the phone. "I better go. But plan some manicures or facials or something for all of us after I arrive. My treat, okay? Least I can do since I've been a deadbeat maid of honor."

"You're not a deadbeat," Maeve lied. "But I could sure use a manicure. Thanks, Vi." Maeve turned off her phone, still staring at Lacey's door, hoping she'd step out in something she liked. She glanced at Bess. "Does it really take this long to put on a dress?"

"No kidding," Bess muttered. "My butt's falling asleep in this chair."

Picking at her fingernails from sheer boredom, Maeve glanced up when she heard the creak of the dressing room door. Looking unimpressed, Lacey moved toward the mirror.

"Isn't that the same dress you had on before?" Bess's tone dripped of sarcasm and Maeve gave her a smack on the leg.

"No," Lacey said defensively. "This one doesn't have that little flower thing on the waist."

Maeve shared a look with Bess, who was biting her lip, probably to keep herself from making another comment.

"Do you like it?" Maeve asked apprehensively. *Please say no.*

"It's tasteful." Lacey's tone was noncommittal. "I could dye it after and probably wear it to a military ball, you know? I kind of like that."

Maeve clenched her hands together, resisting the urge to fly out of her seat and slap some sense into her friend.

Bess's face scrunched up. "Did you really just say that you'd *dye* your wedding dress?"

Lacey's eyes widened. "It's practical. And those ball gowns I have to buy for these military functions get expensive."

"But it's your wedding dress." Bess drew the word "wedding" out to last about three seconds, as though Lacey had never heard the word before.

"And you don't love it, right?" Maeve confirmed.

Lacey looked at herself in the mirror again and shrugged. "No."

"Well, thank God, 'cause I hate it." Maeve stood, giving Lacey a final once-over before heading back to the assortment of gowns they had pulled from the racks. "A wedding gown is something you should love—love enough to not be willing to dye it afterward." She handed the bridal consultant a strapless mermaid gown with a sweetheart neckline. "I'd like to see her in this one next, please."

Lacey gave her head a quick shake. "That one's too princessy for me, Maeve. Too poofy. I'd feel like a meringue."

"Lacey, I love you. But your taste sucks. You don't know what looks good on you. And it's not even a princess style. It's a mermaid."

"And it's a wedding dress," Bess piped in. "There's nothing wrong with a little poof on a wedding dress."

Maeve narrowed her eyes. "Put it on or I'm putting it on you myself. Got it?"

"I'll hold her down while you pull it over her head," Bess volunteered.

Lacey sighed, grumbling something about overbearing bridesmaids as she headed into the dressing room.

Bess snickered as Maeve moved back to her seat. "'Bout time you made her try on something you picked out."

"If I didn't, we'd be here all night and I've got a date."

"With who?"

"Joe. You know, the SEAL CO."

Bess fluttered her hand to her chest. "Be still my heart. Another SEAL for us to entertain on Scrabble nights? Just promise me I can still live in your house after you've married him."

"Not bloody likely. Mick told me he's been married twice. If two divorce decrees hasn't soured him to marriage, I don't know what would." A smile hitched up on Maeve's face. "I'll just have to use him for sex."

"What a chore, huh?" Bess laughed.

Maeve glanced over her shoulder to the selection of bridesmaid gowns. "Want to check out something for us while she's changing?"

Bess followed her to a rack packed with a rainbow of brightly colored gowns. "Sure. Did Vi give us the go-ahead to pick something out?" Gazing at the price tag of the first one she found, she bit her lip.

"Yep. And a bonus for the person who finds her a maid of honor dress. A case of Merlot."

"If I win, can I trade it in for baby food?"

"I'm sure that would be fine with her." Maeve reached for the tag on a dress. "The prices are great here." She had hoped Lacey would get lucky and find a dress sample at one of the boutiques they had tried. But Maeve had to admit that this warehouse-like store, though lacking in ambiance, really did have a good selection of reasonable gowns.

"Yeah," Bess replied in a quiet voice. "I just see numbers and calculate how many diapers that buys."

"I'll cover whatever you can't."

Bess looked annoyed by the offer. "No, you won't. You cover too much already. And you don't even have a job now, Maeve. I've got to start acting like a responsible mother, rather than your coddled friend."

"I don't coddle you."

"Yes, you do. And I love you for it. But I'll be damned if I can't buy a dress for her wedding on my own."

"Okay, okay." Breezing her hand against the flurry of price tags dangling from the rack, Maeve was drawn to a number so low she was almost too scared to pull the gown from the rack. She eyed the dress, pleasantly surprised, picturing how the right accessories might make it look designer chic rather than knockoff cheap. "What do you think of this one? We could see if they have it in red, to match some of the roses in our bouquets."

Bess nervously bit her lip. "I like it." Hesitantly, she took the price tag in hand and beamed. "I like it a lot."

"Let's see what Lacey says." Maeve glanced over at the door to the dressing room and saw her friend emerging, a smile on her face.

A sweetheart neckline punctuated with crystals cascaded to a dropped waist accentuating Lacey's curves. Flowing layers of organza swirled downward, embellished with delicate lace appliques. Her cheeks were flushed, and her eyes welled up with a sheen of tears as she looked at herself in the mirror.

"What do you think?" Maeve asked, and held her breath.

"I love it," Lacey said, looking as though she didn't believe the words would ever come from her mouth. "It's not at all what I was picturing. But I feel like—"

"A bride?" Maeve offered.

"Yeah. A bride."

Bess grinned. "And you could dye it after for a ball."

Lacey held her hands to the front of the dress protectively. "Over my dead body."

Triumphant, Maeve looked at the bridal consultant. "We'll take it."

CHAPTER 7

Joe stood as Maeve approached the table. "For the record, when I offer to buy a woman dinner, I'm willing to spring for more than burgers," he offered as he pulled out her chair.

Maeve smiled as she drank in the sight of him in uniform. His chest was adorned with so many more service ribbons than Jack, or even Mick. "I'm sure you are. But I was in the mood for burgers and they've got the best."

Their small table was set against a window overlooking a side street off Main. Quaint historic row houses with colorful trim lined the lamp-lit street, and tourists darted off to their hotels, or out for a night in one of Annapolis's ample selection of pubs.

Following Maeve's gaze, his eyes were drawn to the view. "I know. I used to go here during my Academy days." He glanced downward. "I don't think they've cleaned the floors since then."

Laughing, Maeve took the menu from the waitress. "I hope I'm not late."

"You're right on time. I'm early. I had a late meeting at Fort Meade, but didn't have enough time to change, so thought I'd come straight here." He cocked his head apologetically, and his smile was nothing less than intoxicating. "Sorry about the uniform. Of course, Mick would probably bet I sleep in the damn thing."

Maeve's lips curved a touch upward. Mick had said something to that effect. "He only had good things to say about you. But from his description, I think I might tell you that you work too hard."

"Goes with this," he said, pointing to his command pin. "But when I retire at thirty years, I plan on never answering another email. And I'm never shaving again."

She tried to picture it. Even at seven o'clock the man didn't have a speck of stubble on his strong, angular jawline. He probably shaved in between meetings, just so he could be as much the perfect officer at night as he was first thing in the morning. "And the high and tight? Getting rid of that, too?"

He ran his fingers through his short, cropped hair. "You think this is a high and tight? You don't see enough Marines. I'd need to cut it a quarter inch shorter for that. But your idea's not that bad, actually. Maybe I'll grow it long. Start a garage band."

"Do you play an instrument?"

"Not a damn one. No time for it. But I've been told the way my fingers play the M240 machine gun, I might have some promise with a guitar."

Maeve laughed, surprised by how easily conversation flowed in Joe's presence as they chatted about everything from the best way to grill a burger to where to find the friendliest people in Europe.

Some men knew a little bit about everything, just to keep a conversation going. Joe seemed to know a lot about everything. And she didn't hesitate to tell him so. "Is that from traveling so much with the Navy?" she asked.

"A little. But mostly it's from reading. When I'm deployed, there's lot of prep time, training for a mission. But then there are these long lulls while you wait for the green light. I like to read then— open my mind to history and the ideas of other cultures." He scoffed. "I try to make my men do the same, but they'd rather pick up an iPad and play a game."

They ordered their meals and Maeve relished in hearing about his travels. She had been to France twice, but that was the limit of her European explorations. Italy, she made a mental note. She would see Italy next, she decided as she listened intently to him describe a NATO training operation he led along the Cinque Terre coast.

Comfortable, she leaned back in her chair, letting the oaky Merlot that Joe had selected for her send a warm sensation through her body.

For a woman who was described by her friends as a serial dater, Maeve actually hated dating. Men would just stare at her, so fixated on the superficial, and Maeve would always be the one carrying the conversation. How refreshing it was to spend time with a man who had opinions about something other than football, and ambitions broader than just wanting a bigger TV than his buddies.

"So why were you in Paris? Work or play?" he asked.

"It's impossible to go to Paris for work and not at least play a little."

"True."

Maeve toyed with the stem of the wineglass, remembering. "But it was mostly work last time I went. The firm had a client who demanded everything be completely unique and direct from France. They were the most obsessive, spoiled, and impossible couple to work with. But seeing as I got a free trip to France out of the deal, they still go down as my favorite clients."

"Impressive."

"How so?"

"You must be good at what you do to travel at someone else's expense."

Maeve shrugged. "I used to think so. Maybe I got a bit too cocky, though, because I quit my job and now I'm flailing around, trying to figure out my next move. My friends have been pushing me to open my own company rather than work for someone else. It's riskier than I usually like things. Takes luck, too, and I may have already used up my share of that."

"If luck were something you could run out of, I'd be dead by now, Maeve." His cell rang, and he reached into his pocket to silence it. "I'd love to see some of your work."

"I actually just put up a website. Well, my friend Bess did, actually. And Jack convinced me to do a few Navy families' houses pro bono, just to get some publicity."

"Jack." He leaned back. "You mean Falcone?"

Maeve nodded. "He tells me you Navy people have a hard time decorating houses since you move so much."

"He's damn right about that. A 3,500 square foot house came with my command and I have furniture in just two rooms. It's ridiculous. Guess they assume that anyone at my rank should have a wife and three kids by now." He laughed, taking a sip of his beer. "Two ex-wives was the best I could do."

"If you take some pictures of your rooms, I can give you some advice."

"I'd love that. As CO, I'm expected to host a lot of socials, and I can't do that on a futon." His finger toyed with the condensation on the bottle of Arrogant Bastard. "And he's right. Word spreads in Annapolis. The locals love a good Navy story."

"I hope so. But in the meantime, it just makes me feel good to be doing something for these families. I mean, I know it's just throw pillows and some paint, but to make a house feel like home…"

"Don't undersell how much it means to come home to a welcoming place when you've been at sea for six months," he interrupted. "So you and Jack. What's the deal there?"

"Jack? Oh, I've known him since forever. Feels like that anyway. He's—like my brother."

Joe laughed. "Christ, don't tell him that."

"What?"

"I saw the way he looked at you that day in front of Rickover Hall. And it's not like a brother. You didn't just drop out of a stork's basket. You should know that."

Maeve sighed. "Well, there might be remnants of something. We—dated briefly a long time ago." *Dated?* Maeve nearly laughed. She and Jack had shared a weekend of unbridled sex. There had been no dates involved. She cleared her throat awkwardly. "But we're just friends now. We want different things."

"You and all men. Men want a good steak, sex, and a remote with fresh batteries. Of course you want something different. You're a woman."

"I meant the bigger picture. Future. Kids."

"Do me a favor and don't tell him that right now."

"Why?"

"Because where he's headed, he should keep his optimism up." He paused only long enough for a chill to shoot up her spine. "So you do or don't want kids?"

"They're not in my plans," she answered vaguely.

"I'm with you there. After three commands, I feel like I already raised enough children."

"How about getting married again?" she asked.

"Thanks for the offer, but it's just our first date."

Maeve laughed. "Seriously, do you think you'll try again one day?"

"They say three's a charm. But I'm definitely waiting till I get out of the Navy. We have a saying, 'If the military wanted you to have a wife, they would have issued you one.'"

Maeve tilted her head. "Some marriages survive it. So what's their secret? With Mick marrying my best friend, I better have some advice to give him."

"You're asking the wrong man. Two divorces, remember?"

"That should make you the expert. You know what not to do."

Joe looked thoughtful for a moment. "I guess the key is not to make too many withdrawals."

"Excuse me?"

"A marriage is like a bank. You make deposits. You make withdrawals. If you come up too much in the red and can't pull yourself out of debt, you'll be seeing a lawyer."

"I never thought about it that way."

"Being in the service, Mick automatically will be taking plenty of withdrawals out. Missed birthdays and anniversaries. All the stress that comes with being married to a man in the service. So I'd tell Mick that when he is home—when he's actually around—make plenty of deposits. I didn't do that. When I was stateside, I was still working the long hours and away too much. I focused on my career 365 days a year."

"But it got you a command."

"Yep. And promoted early three times in a row." He took a sip of beer. "And divorced twice, which isn't something I'd recommend to Mick."

"Me neither," she agreed, tucking away his advice for the next time she saw Mick.

As Maeve shut the front door gently behind her, she could still feel the warmth of his kiss on her lips, even though at least fifteen minutes had passed since he had walked her to her car.

The man oozed sex appeal, and it was a wonder Maeve hadn't invited him home with her. God knows it had been ages since she'd had sex and she couldn't help the curiosity of what might lie beneath that perfectly starched uniform.

With her body still humming from the energy of good conversation and healthy flirtation, she ventured to the back porch to relax.

Joe Shey. The man was an enigma. A bod molded from steel. Sense of humor, and eyes that generated an electric charge. Smart. Funny.

How the hell could he be twice divorced? Were the women on crack?

Swinging the back door open just as her nose noticed the curious smell of something burning, she saw Bess and Lacey sitting on the deck, armed with hot glue guns. "Hey. I hope you guys weren't waiting up for me."

Lacey's face scrunched as she squeezed the gun, making a line of glue along the rim of a candle votive. "Don't flatter yourself. We're still trying to finish this brilliant idea you had for adorning these stupid candle holders."

Bess handed Lacey a piece of red ribbon. "Temper, temper. They'll look pretty when they're done."

"Sure, but my carpal tunnel is killing me."

Maeve slipped off her heels—God, they made her feet hurt now that she had become so accustomed to Lacey's borrowed flats. Sitting at the table, she outstretched her hand. "Here. I'll take over."

Relief breezed over Lacey's face. "Thanks. I need some aspirin. I'll be right back."

"How'd the date go?" Bess handed Maeve a fresh glue stick to load the gun.

Maeve looked at the cream-colored stick, baffled. She had never been the crafty type. "Fine. Perfect, really." It had been the perfect date. Lively conversation, never waning, with a man she could easily let herself get wrapped up in like a spicy enchilada.

"Fine? Or perfect? Because there's a world of difference between the two."

"I don't know. He's—an incredible man. There's nothing lacking. But he's just not—"

"—Jack," Bess finished for her.

Lacey popped back through the door. "Jack? What about Jack? Did I miss something?"

Bess grinned. "Maeve was just telling us how she would have rather been out with Jack this evening."

Maeve cocked her head to the side. "Rewind. I did not just say that. If I recall, my exact words were something like Joe Shey is an incredible man. The only person who mentioned Jack is Bess."

Lacey nodded sagely at Bess. "Jack is pretty amazing. He's like one of those superheroes. Nerdy brain-boy by day. Saves the country by night. Mmm."

Bess raised her eyebrows. "Don't forget you're engaged."

Lacey snorted. "Just 'cause a girl is engaged doesn't mean she can't point out the good thing her friend is *completely* ignoring."

Furrowing her brow as she squeezed her gun against a votive, Bess glanced up. "True."

Maeve crossed her arms. "So I take it you don't want to hear about my date with Joe."

Bess shrugged. "You're home by eleven. We're guessing there's not much to report."

Damn. Maeve hated it when someone over a decade younger than her was completely right... again.

"Are you going to see him again?" Lacey asked.

"Sure I will, but—"

"—probably more as a friend," Bess finished for her.

"Yeah." Maeve's mouth pinched downward on one side. "Honestly, I don't think he even seemed that into me. We just weren't clicking in... that way."

Lacey set down a completed votive, admiring her work. "Captain Shey's been around the block, Maeve. He's not the younger guy you usually date. He could probably tell your heart wasn't in it."

"Yeah. Maybe. I don't know what's wrong with me, though. He's everything I should be attracted to. He's perfect for me." Maeve puffed out her cheeks and let out a slow breath. "There's something wrong with me."

"The only thing that is wrong is that you're in love with Jack, and you're trying to date someone else."

"You mistake lust for love."

Bess and Lacey exchanged a glance.

"Okay. I love Jack," Maeve conceded, "but I'm not in love with him."

Bess sighed. "Maeve, you started falling in love that moment you laid eyes on him in O'Toole's, and now you're a hundred feet deep in it."

Maeve set down the glue gun and flicked the switch off. "Well, I better climb my way out of it, because he's not for me." Pressing her fingers against her temples, she rose. "Lacey, where's that aspirin?"

CHAPTER 8

Jack bounded down the steps from a home that bordered the grounds of the Academy's Worden Field. His eyes were drawn to Maeve's sassy stride two steps ahead of him, and an appreciative smile crept up his face.

Damn, she was a sight in her snug pencil skirt and light blouse that fluttered in the tiniest breeze. "So, what do you think? Can you do something for him?" he asked.

It had been harder than he had suspected to find someone willing to take him up on an offer of a free interior designer. Most guys he ran into at work were pretty content with their bland décor. But Logan, a freshly promoted Lieutenant Commander who had just PCSed from California, seemed pretty happy with the deal when he first laid eyes on Maeve.

His possessive side bearing its ugly head, Jack frowned at the memory of how Logan had looked at her. Jack's reaction had been nothing less than caveman.

Oblivious, Maeve practically skipped down the brick walkway. "He doesn't have many accent pieces to work with. Really nice books though. I've got to find a good way to display them. They just shouldn't be boxed up like that. His sofa's pretty tired, but with a slipcover and a few pillows on it, it will be good as new." Still walking, she turned to Jack. "What is it with you guys and sofas? Yours looks like it came from—"

"—Craigslist. I know. You've told me already."

"Oh." Maeve looked nonplussed. "Blue seems to be his favorite color."

"That goes with being in the Navy."

"But the house is too dark for me to use too much. I'm thinking a textured cream with gold accents would work better."

Her stride was quicker these days now that she seemed to favor flats instead of heels. He enjoyed the new look, simply because of the way her hips now swayed swiftly as her long legs flew along the tree-lined sidewalk two steps ahead of him again.

He must look as pathetic as he felt sometimes with her—following her around like a puppy dog. Eager for any scrap she sent his way. Purposefully, he picked up his pace. "He'll like that since he graduated here. Blue and gold are our colors."

"He's cute, too. I'll definitely take some pictures of him sitting in his place when I'm done with it. It'll look great on my blog. Ugh. Who came up with that word, anyway? 'Blog.' Sounds like something bad. 'I'd love to go to the party, but I've got a touch of the blog.'"

Jack barely heard her. "You think he's cute?"

Maeve froze and studied him, a pert smile creeping up her face. "What? Are you jealous?"

"Of course not." He hated that she noticed. It was pitiful enough to have traded Bess fifteen babysitting hours for information on what time Maeve got home from her date. Eleven, Jack had been thrilled to hear. "You just talk about men like they're pieces of meat. You're a chauvinist."

Maeve shrugged, as if to say, "Tell me something I don't know already," and continued walking toward his truck. "And his whole story about wanting to adopt a dog, but not being able to because he's always deploying? That couldn't be any sweeter if I topped it with frosting. I've got to work that in to the blog entry, too."

"See? You've got a knack for this."

"And I love that he's a SEAL."

"Former SEAL," Jack corrected.

"I have to put that in there, too. Everyone loves a SEAL, right?"

"I wouldn't know," Jack deadpanned. Having reached his truck, he opened her door for her. "I've got a couple other folks lined up, too. One's got a little girl who has never really had a bedroom that she could decorate because they moved so much."

Maeve's expression warmed. "Aww. I'm going to do something amazing for her. Maybe something princessy or a fairy wonderland, depending on what she likes."

"You might be surprised. She likes astronauts. Not fairies or princesses."

"I'll be damned." She leaned against the truck for a moment thoughtfully, her eyes drifting to the waves beating at the rocks along the Severn River.

Jack resisted the urge to sandwich her between him and his Ford, planting a warm kiss on her lips.

"Good for her," she continued, unaware of his yearnings. "Thanks for driving me. Always a pain to not be able to drive past security."

"Gotta marry military to get in on your own, Maeve."

"Ahh, there's a price for everything." She took a deep breath, seeming to savor the cool breeze blowing off the water. "But to have access to this view, at least I'd get more out of it than my last marriage."

"It is pretty, isn't it?" he agreed. As she climbed into his truck, her skirt hiked up a couple inches and his gaze lingered before he slammed the door shut. *Pretty, indeed.*

Climbing in, he glanced at Maeve. "Hungry?"

"Famished. But I'm not letting Bess cook tonight."

"Something wrong?"

"Abigail was up last night. Bad dream or something. Bess couldn't get back to sleep. She slept on the couch downstairs so she could be close to her crib in case she woke up again." She fastened her seatbelt. "I'm thinking of moving Abigail into Lacey's room after she leaves for San Diego. Then maybe turning the downstairs bedroom into an office for me."

"Love the idea. Let me know when you need to move the furniture and I'll stop by."

"You'll be gone by then, won't you?"

Struck by the reality, he felt an odd sense of loss. "You're right." Who would help Maeve take care of her to-do list when he was gone? Logan, the new Lieutenant Commander with the fresh California tan? Jack's lip curled at the image.

"So anyway, thought we'd order pizza," Maeve said.

"Works for me. Let's pick up a couple pizzas from Donatello's on the way home. They're better than delivery." Eyes locked on the rear view mirror, he pulled out of the tight space, being extra careful as he noticed the DoD sticker with stars on the windshield of the car behind him. Best not to bump the car of an Admiral.

"Still up to putting the arbor together tonight?" she asked.

"I better be. Wedding's around the corner. We can't count on many more clear nights and we still need to stain it. We're pushing things enough already. I think all my sisters have started a betting pool about whether or not we can pull off a wedding on such short notice."

"We'll pull it off."

Donatello's was a short drive off base, and they lucked out with parking, sliding into a space right in front of the door.

Maeve glanced at her watch after they made their order standing in front of the cash register. "Thirty minutes till it's ready? I'm dying here," she commented.

"Let's grab a table out front and get an appetizer while we wait." They stepped into the fresh spring air again and grabbed the last table for two. Donatello's outdoor seating was slim, a few tiny tables overlooking Spa Creek. He pulled a chair out for Maeve.

"This is a nice view for a pizza place. You've been here before, I take it?"

Jack nodded. "Best pizza in Naptown. And my Italian father agrees with me. We came here on our first trip to Annapolis to check out the Academy back when I was in high school." He smiled at the memory. "Want a glass of wine?"

"You know, I think I will. I feel kind of like celebrating."

"I like the sound of that. What are we celebrating?"

"My first client as an independent designer. And I might have two drinks so that I forget that I'm doing it for free." She laughed. "Do they have a wine list?"

Jack snorted. "This is a pizza joint, Maeve. It's white or red here."

Maeve rolled her eyes lavishly. "You do spoil a girl, Jack," she said sarcastically.

"I save the spoiling for the women I'm dating. You've made it pretty clear you're not going to be one of them."

The light that he had seen in her eyes extinguished, and he immediately regretted saying it, though he had no idea why the words had struck her the wrong way.

When the waitress appeared, Jack ordered drinks and appetizers.

Maeve pressed her lips together thoughtfully a moment, and then said, "Mick finally found a Navy chaplain who wasn't booked that Saturday."

"I didn't know he was having trouble with that."

"Oh, yeah. Lacey was so worried. Wanted me to look into getting ordained so I could do the ceremony myself."

Jack burst out laughing.

"Why is that so funny?"

"The idea of you standing in front of a bunch of people and talking about marriage. You trash-talk the institution like a gifted pro."

"Do I?"

"Hell, yeah."

Her face fell. "How awful. I really should watch that. Especially with the wedding coming up. Do me a favor and smack me on the shoulder or something if I do it again, okay?"

"It will be my pleasure." He gave her arm a supportive squeeze, because she looked like she needed it.

"Oh—and we've got the florist booked. They're wonderful, Jack." She absently took his hand in excitement and just as the warmth of her skin had soaked in, she pulled her hand away. "They even came out to the house to see what flowering plants would be in bloom in June so that they can be sure to match the setting."

Jack sighed. "Maeve, let's stop talking about the wedding."

She looked perplexed. "What do you want to talk about then?"

"Anything. Just not the wedding. It's bad enough I'll be spending my Thursday night staining a wedding arbor we could have lived without."

"Hey. You said the arbor was gorgeous."

"Great. I said it was great," he clarified. No straight man alive would refer to an inanimate object as gorgeous. Maeve was gorgeous. The arbor was great. "But we could have lived without it."

"I just want it to be perfect for her."

"It will be perfect." He took her hand. "It will be perfect if you stop stressing out about making it perfect. You're going to wear yourself out worrying."

"Point taken." She glanced at her watch. "No wedding talk for the next 20 minutes till the pizza comes."

"Good. All my sisters are married. This is my third time being best man, and my eighth being a groomsman. I even walked one of my sisters down the aisle when my dad was recovering from open heart surgery. I'm pretty much wedding-ed out."

"I didn't know that." She glanced up from her wine glass. "About your dad."

"See? That's just it. I've probably spent more time with you than any woman in my life except blood relations. But we rarely really talk."

"Is he okay now?"

"Healthy as a horse. Scared two years of life off my mother though. It happened a week before my sister's wedding and she wanted to postpone, but my dad wouldn't allow it. He's as stubborn as a mule."

When the waitress brought them their appetizers, Jack ordered two more to go.

Maeve's eyes widened. "Hungry a little?"

"I might not be stateside much longer. I want to enjoy real food while I can. You can't get mozzarella balls and antipasti in an MRE."

"Are you excited to go?"

Jack opened his mouth to answer, and then shut it, looking out to the view of the water. "Not this time, no." Tentatively, he took a long pull of his beer. His eyes met hers and he soaked in her image, memorizing it, and locking it away for later. "I needed more time here."

"For what?"

"I'm thirty. Irish Catholic on one side of the family and Italian Catholic on the other. The last in my family to not get married. So you know I catch a lot of flack about it. But I've been at sea so much, it's kind of hard to meet a soul mate from a sub."

Maeve reached for a calamari. "I can relate to that. There's something about thirty. I was 29 when I got married and I really think I latched on to the wrong guy just because I saw that scary three-zero looming in the distance."

29, he thought. That was right after he had met her, and he wondered if that had anything to do with why she had never called him. A woman on a husband hunt wouldn't want to waste time with a new Academy grad who could only offer her a lengthy long distance relationship.

"And I'm from the South," Maeve continued with a wry smile. "My mother had been planning my wedding since I was two years old, looking at wedding gown magazines in between pageants."

"You were a pageant baby?"

"I have three crowns in my closet."

"All this time, I never knew I was in the company of royalty."

Laughing, she continued. "So anyway, she got what she wanted—big Southern wedding and a big Southern divorce." She sighed, taking another calamari as he extended one toward her. "Pageants back then weren't quite as over the top as they are now. But I definitely shimmered too much for my dad to approve. And Gram—oh, she thought it was a disgrace. She thought little girls should be in lace and silk bows rather than lipstick and bling."

"I have to side with your grandma there."

She grinned, cocking her head to the side as she looked at him, as though a realization was forming in her head. "Gram would have liked you. And not just because your mother's Irish as Paddy's pig. Though that would have earned you major points with her." Her eyes locked with his, and she stared silently at him a little longer than was usual. Leaning back suddenly, she swayed slightly in her chair.

"Are you okay?" Jack touched her arm.

"I'm okay. Just felt a little dizzy there."

"Want to go home? We can forget the pizzas if you're not feeling well."

"No, no. I'm fine." She gave herself a little shake, as though to wake herself up. "Must be this cheap wine they serve here. Tastes like it came from a box."

"It probably did. Here." He loaded her small appetizer plate with calamari, bruschetta, and Carpaccio. "You don't eat enough. My mother would tell me I should fatten you up."

"I like the sound of your mother."

"You'll meet her at the awards ceremony. The whole family is coming down for it."

"Bet you can't wait."

"To see them? Always. But to stand in front of the brigade while they make a big show out of something I'd rather forget? Not excited at all about that."

"Mick says you can't talk about the mission."

Jack nodded. "Not much."

"But you risked your life to save others?"

"Mick tell you that?"

She shook her head. "Just guessed that part. They don't give you awards for serving ice cream."

Jack shrugged.

Maeve swallowed. "Will this next job be something similar?"

"Sure as hell hope not. It's never a good thing when SEALs need someone with nuke expertise. Thought I'd be going back to my boring job on a sub after this."

"Something tells me that being on a sub armed with nuclear warheads is the furthest thing from boring."

"You'd be wrong then." He lifted a bruschetta to his mouth, and noticed her wine glass was nearly empty. "Want another glass?

"No. One's enough for me. And stop putting things on my plate. I have a bridesmaid dress I have to fit into."

"We're not supposed to talk about the wedding, remember?"

"Sorry. It slipped out." She turned her chair toward the view, moving it closer to Jack. He wondered if the closeness was accidental, or whether she too felt the pull to be closer to him just like he felt it for her.

The sloshing of the waves against the shoreline was rhythmic, almost sexual. Snap out of it, he told himself. As the sun lowered in the sky, he longed to be able to take her home to his place, rather than spending the night staining an arbor.

"Beautiful evening," she said, her shoulder lightly touching his arm as she scooted her chair again, gazing out to the water. The sun cast a golden glow on the boats in the water and the clang of the halyards on the sailboats as the wind passed was hypnotic.

When were those damn pizzas going to be ready? Maeve was sitting so close to him he could smell the vanilla lotion she always rubbed into her soft hands, and the scent of her shampoo—or whatever it was she put in her hair to make it look so perfect.

Finishing her glass of wine, a contented grin crept up her face. "This is the first day I actually feel like I might be able to do this. Go out on my own, run a business, you know?"

"Good," his hand gently rubbed her back, strictly a gesture of support, he convinced himself. It had nothing to do with his need to touch her in any way she'd allow him.

"And you did that for me." She turned to him, so close that he could feel a few strands of her hair brush against his neck when a breeze passed.

"Me?"

"You set this up, Jack. All of it. You had Bess put up the website. Came up with the idea for publicity. Arranged for me to meet my first client. Everything. I'd have taken the first job in retail if you hadn't made me so confident I could do this."

"Wait a minute. You got a job offer?"

Maeve nodded. "Yesterday. Selling furniture at the mall. Your basic sales position, but they'd *call* me a designer."

"And you turned it down?"

"Yes." She turned from the view, her face suddenly too close to his.

"That's my girl!" Impulsively, he kissed her briefly on the lips, a kiss between friends that unwittingly sent a shock of heat to his groin. Big mistake. *Gentlemen, start your engines.*

He pulled back, a smile frozen on his face that he hoped masked his sudden urge to cement his body against hers. "You did the right thing. I'm proud of you."

Her eyes were still locked on his and her smile slowly faded. He wondered for a moment if she was feeling another wave of dizziness till she raised both her hands to his cheeks and leaned in to him.

It was barely even a kiss at first, a tentative grazing of her lips against his. The moment was in slow motion for Jack, something he had imagined for so long that his brain slowed each millisecond down so that he could savor it. Then his breath caught as suddenly her mouth urged him on.

Her hands traced along his face down to his neck, her touch sending his heart into sixth gear. Not stopping to think, his hands found the nape of her neck, and moved slowly, cradling her face as though she were a precious, fragile crystal. Her tongue touched his, the tang of cheap wine mixed with the sweet, salty taste that was unique to Maeve. Her palms were so soft, still stroking his face, pulling him closer, urging him to not stop. The feel of her hands—so supple—kneading into his hair brought a wave of memories of her hands on other places on his body.

Finally.

He'd die for this woman. He'd give his last breath to have her beneath him right now. Damn the pizzas and the arbor. He'd lift her out of her chair and carry her two miles to his home right now if she'd let him.

A fire surged inside him, toasting his body like a hot kiln, making him desperate to be alone with her. His hands travelled to her waist as he explored her with his mouth, pulling her closer, tighter, fighting the urge to pull her onto his lap. His lips still melded with hers, he leaned in, his hand at her back as he pulled her body closer to his. His body responded to the feel of her breasts pressing up against him, until she suddenly pulled back so quickly she nearly fell off her chair.

Her one hand covered her lips and her other she held against her chest. "Oh, God, I'm sorry, Jack."

Sorry? She was sorry? "Don't say that, Maeve." His hands were still in her hair. God, her hair. He had forgotten how soft it was to hold. Had it really been eight years since he had enjoyed the feeling of those soft strands caressing his fingers?

"I shouldn't have done that."

He dropped his hands. "Christ. Tell me you're joking, Maeve. It was good. We're good. We're good together."

"We can't be together that way." Maeve looked away.

He wouldn't let her drop it. Not this time. "Give me one reason."

Her eyes filled with tears and it tore at his soul.

"It's just… it just won't work, Jack. I don't want to start something with you that would only end badly."

"You're killing a relationship before it even started then."

"But I could never make you happy. We want different things. And then we'd end up breaking up—and then I'd lose you."

He took her face in his hands. "You're not going to lose me. Just give us a chance."

"Please. Please, can we just stay friends?"

Bewildered, Jack barely acknowledged boxes of take-out that were plopped in front of them by the waitress with a bill on top. He just stared at Maeve. "Friends are honest with each other, Maeve. And if you can't tell me what's really holding you back, then I can't say that we're really friends, can I?"

Maeve's eyes dropped. "I'm sorry." Her voice was barely a whisper as she reached for her purse.

He snatched the bill from the top of the boxes and handed the waitress his credit card.

"So. Are you going to tell me what the hell that was all about?" Barely a second had passed since Bess had shut the door on Lacey, Mick, and Jack. She glared at Maeve.

"What do you mean?" Maeve tried to sound innocent, even though she knew she couldn't fool Bess. She could have cut the tension in her house that night with a knife, and considered herself lucky that Lacey had gone home with Mick, or she'd have two people interrogating her right now.

"You and Jack barely said a word to each other all night. You barely looked at each other, for that matter. Did you two have an argument or something?"

Maeve stalked into the kitchen as Bess followed. "Or something." Glancing down at the wood stain that had dyed her fingertips, she started to scrub them again. Having a flashback to her freshman English class, she felt a little like Lady Macbeth with blood on her hands, trying to wash it away—hoping it would erase her mistake this past evening.

Out, out, damn spot!

"Spill it, Maeve."

Maeve scrunched a dishtowel in her hands and hung it on the refrigerator. "I kissed Jack."

A smile exploded on Bess's face. "About time. So that's good, right? I mean, why did you guys not even speak to each other tonight?"

"Because I shouldn't have. He just looked so damn cute sitting there at the restaurant while we waited for the pizza. And he's so great—been so supportive of me trying to start a business and all. It was appreciation. That's what it was."

"Appreciation? Bullshit." Her voice was low to not wake Abigail or let her hear her mother's more colorful language.

"And attraction. I'll admit that. God, the man kisses like he invented the act." Her eyes drifted, lost in the memory. "So anyway, there we were, waiting for the pizzas, enjoying this romantic view. And all of a sudden I just plaster myself against him. I attacked him really. I don't know what got into me. Cheap wine, probably."

"And then? I'm waiting to hear when this all turned into a bad thing."

"Then he pulls me closer. You know, right up against him. And I suddenly feel my rock-hard implants encased in years of scar tissue, pressing against his chest. Damn things are like baseballs. I'd be surprised if he didn't notice." Her face was sullen as she sank into the sofa. "I jumped back. It's like I just suddenly remembered that I wasn't the Maeve he knew eight years ago." She buried her face in her hands. "He must have thought I was nuts."

"Oh, Maeve. Who the hell cares about your damn implants. Half the women of America have them, for God's sake. Or at least half the ones who can fill out a bikini do."

"Yeah, but they don't have all the baggage that goes with them. Cancer. Bad eggs. No kids. I just don't want to have the Big Talk with him, you know? That would ruin everything."

"You're a cock tease."

"I am not," Maeve denied.

"Well, you're the closest thing. Hell, even I'm mad at you. You guys are supposed to be together. Everyone who gets within a five-mile radius of you two can feel it."

"I had my chance with Jack."

"And you got a second chance. It's a freaking miracle, Maeve. Think about it. You fell hard for him eight years ago. Admit it."

"Who wouldn't? But he wasn't ready for a serious relationship back then. And that's what I was looking for."

"And then you end up inheriting a house here in Annapolis, and moving in with the woman who was destined to be Jack's best friend's fiancée. What are the chances?"

"Slim to none," Maeve admitted.

"It's destiny."

Maeve rolled her eyes as she settled into the plush back cushions of the sofa. "Gram used to say that destiny sometimes needs a push."

"So, give it a push."

"Last time I gave destiny a push I found myself married to an idiot, in a dead-end job, and rebuilding my life after cancer as a divorcée. Think I'll take logic and free will over destiny any day."

"You are meant to be together." She sat across from Maeve, eyes locked on her.

"Jack is meant to be with someone who can give him kids. And I love him too much to see him give up his dream on a chewed-up cancer survivor who still worries what the next day will bring."

"That's the first time I heard you admit it."

"What? That I'm chewed-up?"

"That you love him."

"Of course I do. I'm not stupid. We might have a good month or two together, but we'd only end up breaking up in the end. I can't live my life thinking that he compromised just so that he could be with me."

Bess stood, tugging firmly on Maeve's arm till she rose from the sofa.

"What?" Maeve whined.

"Come here," Bess said, pushing Maeve in front of the mirror in the entryway. "Look at yourself. How the hell would anyone have to compromise on anything to be with you?"

Maeve's shoulders sagged. "I don't know what to do, Bess."

"You have to at least tell him. Stop trying to protect all of us all the time."

"But I don't want his pity."

"You have a choice. Take the chance on his pity, or let him feel rejected and hurt. Because I guarantee that's what he's feeling right now."

"This sucks, Bess."

"I know, hon. I know." She put her arm around Maeve. Then she let out a snort.

"What?"

"Bet your boobs weren't the only thing hard when you kissed him."

The laugh that escaped Maeve was like a pressure valve. She laughed, until she cried.

CHAPTER 9

"...with complete disregard to his own safety..."

Standing amid the crowd that crushed into O'Toole's that evening as Jack led them in a toast to missing Shipmates, the Admiral's words haunted her.

"...conspicuous gallantry and intrepidity..."

She had stood among the group of civilians in Bancroft Hall at the Academy, beneath the iconic "Don't give up the ship" flag, and watched the brief but awe-inspiring ceremony as they pinned a Silver Star on Jack.

Sandwiched between Bess and Maeve, only a few feet from the swarm of family that Jack had in attendance, she had watched Jack stand at attention, salute, and shake the Admiral's hand as he accepted his award. To their right, Midshipmen stood in formation.

The words of the Admiral were cryptic, barely revealing what Jack had done that day. But Maeve could feel the weight of it bearing down on her heart.

Jack could have died that day—God knows where, doing God knows what to protect our country—and rather than saving himself, he went into the line of fire to save two other men and the mission.

It didn't surprise her. But it troubled her, with words from the Admiral's speech still stirring her mind. She had felt stunningly inadequate standing there in Bancroft Hall, a coward among the brave. A sense of shame had crept into her heart and stayed there even now, as she lifted her glass of Pinot at O'Toole's at the end of the toast.

Missing shipmates, she pondered as she took a long sip, hoping the alcohol might numb the fear that gripped her.

Please God let it not be Jack next.

Jack had done a thorough job of ignoring Maeve the past two days, not that she'd made it difficult. Every waking minute, her finger itched to call him, text him, email him—some form of communication to bridge the icy silence between them. But she had resisted. What was there to say?

Just everything, she answered herself, frowning into her drink.

"You look a million miles away."

Joe's voice startled her, but she was grateful to have been freed from the gloom that seemed to be burying her alive. He was dressed in his choker whites, each medal on his chest shimmering in the low light of the bar. God, he was delectable. But he wasn't Jack.

She shook her head as he extended a stick of fried cheese her way. "Just feeling... I don't know."

Joe nodded. "I've seen that look before. I was married twice, remember? You're in love with him."

Maeve didn't answer. Couldn't. She couldn't admit the truth to someone she didn't know that well, but there was something about Joe Shey that made it impossible to lie to him.

"You're scared for him," Joe continued. "I saw the expression on your face when they pinned that Silver Star on him. I used to get the same look from my exes at these ceremonies, and every damn day I was stateside for that matter. That look that says, 'Don't come home to me in a body bag.' But you have to remember, Jack's well trained. He's damn good at what he does."

"Whatever the hell that is—" Maeve interjected.

"And he's got a good team surrounding him. The best at what they do." He glanced over his shoulder. "Does he know?"

"Know what?"

"That you're in love with him."

The need to flee was overwhelming. That single question was suffocating. So easy to answer, but impossible to act upon. "No."

"Maeve, I'm not one to be romantic. Standing in front of a judge twice and getting handed two divorce decrees will do that to a man." He rested his arm on her shoulder briefly as he turned Maeve to face Jack who was standing across the room. "But that guy over there who just got awarded the Silver Star looks like he just watched his dog get run over by a car. I'm betting you have something to do with that."

Maeve looked at Jack, his eyes empty as he talked to the family and friends around him. The smile on his face was fake; Maeve knew him long enough to know that for a fact.

She had to tell him. She had no right to let him think she was rejecting him. She'd have to take his pity. Stand up to him and make sure he knew he deserved something better. Fight to resume the friendship they had spent the last two years building. And one day, she'd tell him how happy she was to see him settle down and start the family he longed for with someone else.

If she loved him, she had to do that.

Courage. The room, filled with uniforms, was filled with courage. *Let me steal some of that tonight.*

But right now, the crowd and the noise were swallowing her whole. Darting Joe a look just this side of sheer panic, she said, "I have to get out of here."

"You sure?"

"Yeah. But Lacey drove me."

"Need me to drive you home?"

"Please." She glanced over at Lacey across the bar, and made a gesture to the exit, then pointed to Joe. Lacey's eyes widened, and she mouthed, "Don't go."

Maeve shook her head in response, and mouthed back, "I'm okay," as she followed Joe out the door.

The stars twinkled above her, somehow offering her courage. Maeve swayed back and forth in Jack's hammock in his backyard. She had been there for at least an hour, waiting. Long enough that she should feel anxious for him to pull up in the driveway.

Truth was, she was dreading it.

Joe had been blessedly silent when he drove her home from O'Toole's that evening. When he pulled into the driveway, he had only said in a tone she imagined he used with the men he commanded, "Whatever you're planning on doing tonight, don't talk yourself out of it. I've seen a few more years of life than you, Maeve. And I've seen a whole lot more death. Don't let things go unsaid."

Especially not now, Maeve knew he was really saying. With Jack headed out with the SEALs, now was not the time to hold back anything.

So she had grabbed her keys the moment she stepped in her door and drove to Jack's. He was still at O'Toole's, she figured, and she only hoped he would come home alone, or it would make her loitering on his hammock even harder to explain.

Deep breaths. In. Out. She urged herself to be calmed by the peacefulness of the late night. She could hear the Northern spring peepers singing their song—such a lovely sound from a frog, Maeve always thought. More melodic than crickets, the sound lulled her as the hammock rocked in the wind. She dared to shut her eyes, drifting, dreamless...

…till Jack's voice awakened her.

"Maeve? Wake up."

Confused for only a moment, Maeve wondered how many minutes or hours had passed. "Jack. You're home."

"And you're sleeping in my hammock. Are you okay?"

"Yes." For a brief second, courage left her and she struggled to come up with an excuse. "I mean, no. I mean—I really need to talk to you."

He looked quizzical… and tired. She imagined he hadn't planned on having company over at this hour after a long celebration with friends and family downtown.

"I could come back some other time," she offered.

"No. Now's fine. Come on in." He led her inside his apartment and cleared a few things from his couch so she could sit down. "What's going on, Maeve?"

"I—I've felt really badly about the other night."

"Maeve, don't. I'm over it."

"No, stop. Don't give me a way out. I have to tell you this, and it's hard enough."

"What is it?"

"I haven't been honest about why I didn't want a relationship with you, Jack." She started to stand wanting to put some distance between them, but felt weakness in her knees and sat back down.

"Do you want something to drink? Some water?"

"No. What I want is to get through this speech I've got planned, but I can't seem to even start."

She swallowed hard. "I'm—I'm not the same person I was eight years ago, Jack."

"I hope not. Me neither. It's a lot of years."

Maeve didn't know any way of saying it except in one breath. "I'm a cancer survivor."

Jack's brow furrowed. "What?"

"Breast cancer. I was diagnosed with breast cancer about five years ago. I had a double mastectomy, radiation, three rounds of chemo, reconstructive surgery."

"Oh my God, Maeve."

"Yeah, so I'm—you know—not who I once was."

Jack sat in silence a moment, bewildered, till he finally broke the silence. "Why didn't you tell me?"

"I don't know. I liked—us, you know? I liked the way things were. I liked having you think that I was still that 29-year-old. You know. Perfect."

"Is that really what you think of me? You think I'd care?" He took her hands in his own. "God, Maeve, do you really think that I'm attracted to your beauty now? I mean, when I was 22, by God, I'll admit that's all there was for the first night. But even back then, it didn't take me long to figure out that the best part of you is in here." He touched his hand to her heart.

Her breath caught at his touch. "Yeah, but look at you, Jack. You got better with age. Geez, you're twice as wide, but in a good way. And I don't even think that qualifies as a six-pack anymore. More like an eight-pack. And I got—"

"Better," he finished for her. "Stronger. More compassionate and sensitive. Smarter. You're a survivor now. Do you know how sexy that is?"

Maeve was unconvinced.

"Let me show you something." He took off his shirt and her heart rate tripled. He turned to reveal his back, pointing to a scar she had never noticed before among the ripples of muscle. "From shrapnel in my side. My first Purple Heart when I went to Afghanistan."

"I didn't know you got a Purple Heart."

"It's on my uniform. And this one," he said, leading Maeve's hand to his side, "was from that day on the sub. Now I can say I've got a Silver Star to go along with my kick-ass scar."

Maeve bit her lip, not anxious to lift her hand from his body.

"This one," he began, pointing out one on his lower hip, just low enough along his waistband that Maeve's eyes couldn't help drift a little further downward. "Ordnance accident while I was in training." He sat beside her again. "Call me crazy, but I'm pretty damn proud of my scars. And I'll tell you, women seem to find them sexy as hell."

She could imagine. And she preferred not to.

"So I showed you mine. You show me yours." His words were playful, but there was nothing but seriousness in his eyes.

Pressing her lips together, she fought the urge to flee. She wanted to do this, wanted to show him what the years had done to her. She wanted to gain strength from sharing with a man she cared for so deeply.

Tentatively, she pulled the scoop of her dress's neckline down to reveal a small scar just above her breast. "This is my port scar. It's how they delivered the chemo."

Jack touched it reverently, and leaned forward, pressing his lips to the scar and holding them there a moment. "I'm so sorry I wasn't there for you."

Maeve's heartbeat quickened in her chest. Show him, a voice inside her urged. Taking a deep breath, she turned, unzipping the dress halfway, revealing her back. She felt awkward, vulnerable. "Uh, this is where they took some skin for a graft for the reconstructive surgery."

"God, Maeve." He traced a line of kisses along the long faded line of the scar. "It kills me that you went through this." He splayed his hands along her back and stroked her, moving his hands slowly to her sides, and then to her stomach.

Every muscle in her body seized up at his tender touch, and her back arched instinctively.

He kissed her back again, letting his lips linger longer this time, before he lifted his head to speak. "But it only makes you more beautiful. Don't you see that?"

His warm breath as he spoke tickled her back, causing every cell in her body to spark to life. She turned to him now, and his hands never left her body as she slipped her arms out of her sleeves.

With only her bra as a barrier, scars peeked out from beneath the lace. She couldn't quite meet his eyes, which were transfixed on hers waiting for her next words. "The rest are—" She raised one hand to her chest "—here. It's um, a warzone under here." She let out a feeble laugh, trying desperately to make light of the situation.

He stroked her cheek, and touched her bottom lip lightly with his thumb. His touch ventured down her neck, down her chest till he caressed her breasts, fingers tracing the barely visible scars. Lowering his head, he kissed each tiny pink line of flesh with such gentle pressure. She had lost most sensation in her breasts because of the nerve damage from her surgeries, yet somehow, the warmth of his lips aroused her in a way unlike she had ever felt, sending shivers down her spine.

She needed more of this—this acceptance that she hadn't felt from a man since her surgery—this worship of all her flaws as though they were the best part of her.

The air was still as she tentatively reached behind her to unsnap her bra. His hands were swift, yet achingly sweet, as he lifted the material from her body, never letting his lips leave her skin. She could feel his tongue tracing along her reconstructed nipple. How could she feel that? How could she feel the moisture he left behind as he moved his mouth toward the valley between her breasts and climbing again to her next peak? It was as though her nerves had been reawakened, not the same as before her surgery, but alive in a new way, a fascinating way that she wanted to explore more.

Lifting his head from her chest now, he kissed her lips and she leaned into him tentatively, almost fearfully, not wanting their flesh to part, not wanting this to end. Glancing at the lamp momentarily, her hand unconsciously reached for it, wishing she could flick it off and let him imagine her as she once was.

His hand caught hers as he stopped her. "You're more beautiful today than the day I first met you. Everything that you've been through has made you into what you are. And what you are is beautiful."

Blinking back tears, she leaned into him, needing to close the gap between them. His hands held her face as he angled his own toward her, and kissed her in a way that filled in every empty crevasse that had been etched in her soul the past years. He pulled her closer, till her body was on his lap and she could feel the pressure of his erection. Her bare breasts pressed against his chest and she felt a primitive surge from deep within her core.

Oh God, I need this.

He lifted her chin up with his finger, so that their eyes could meet. "What is it you want from me, Maeve? Whatever it is, you have it. My friendship. It's yours. My admiration. Yours. Do you want more?"

Her head swam in emotions, struggling to recall all the reasons she had pushed him away for so long. Yet somehow, now, feeling so gloriously exposed as his tongue traced a path down her neck to her breast, she knew nothing. Nothing except raw need. "I don't know what I want anymore. But I know what I *don't* want."

He lifted his head from breast only a moment. "What's that?"

"I don't want you to stop."

His lips met hers again as he slid his arms beneath her legs and lifted her, carrying her to his bedroom. She felt herself sink into his unmade bed, the coolness of the sheets making her shiver. The small lamp alongside his bed was on, and she reached to turn it off, but he grasped her hand and brought it to his lips. Then he took both her wrists and pinned them in his grasp above her head.

She whimpered helplessly as his free hand slid over her breasts and down to her belly, then beneath her half-removed dress with its silk gathered at her waist. He found the thin fabric of her panties and toyed with the brown curls until he found the tiny nub that, when touched, caused her to arch her body, pressing his hand even closer. His thumb circled as he watched her, seeming to savor the sight of her eyes half shut, her breath quickening.

She struggled to bring her hands to his body, aching to feel him full against her, but his left arm kept her immobile, blessedly trapped.

"Not yet. I want to make you feel just as beautiful as you are," he said, his voice soft, yet demanding. His thumb played and stroked, and his fingers moved between her legs so that he could now feel just how desperately she wanted him. He slipped a finger into her, then another, all the while his thumb still made its circles around her clit.

He let go of her wrists now and moved lower, slipping her dress the rest of the way off her body, along with her panties, in one decisive movement. He kissed her deeply, and Maeve could feel the hard ridge of his arousal pressing into her from beneath his pants. She reached down, longing to have nothing between them, and feel only his skin on hers. "Not yet," he repeated as he moved low on her body again.

"Open for me," he said, his hands lifting her knees upward and splaying her, the cool air meeting her wetness, making her feel even more exposed. His breath met the moisture first, then his fingers, separating her curls and finding the tiny center of her arousal. His lips touched it, then his tongue, so gently, as though she might shatter if he pressed too hard.

And shatter she did. Too soon, too soon, she thought, as her body writhed and bucked beneath his touch. She ached to draw it out as her body climbed further into ecstasy, till she cried out his name, and her body was reduced to complete pliancy.

He grinned up to her. Don't stop, she silently willed him, and he must have read her mind, touching his tongue to her, seeming to delight in the feel of the aftershocks still reverberating inside of her. He slipped his finger inside her as he tasted her—in and out, in and out—the same ancient rhythm her body knew instinctively. She felt sensation build again, slower now, more deliberate, less desperate for climax. In and out, and faster now, the rhythm matched her breathing as it accelerated, her heart pounding beneath her breasts. His one hand slid beneath her butt, pulling her closer, opening her more, making her more and more his with every stroke of his fingers inside her.

"So close, Jack. Please, please, I want you inside of me." Nearly weeping from need, she ached to feel his hardness inside her, deep, as deep as she remembered from eight years ago.

He let her win this time, pulling off his pants and boxers and letting her hand reach out for his hard length. At her slightest touch, his eyes slammed shut and he almost pulled away, as though he had been touched by fire. She reached again, bolder now, gripping him, feeling the blood flow beneath the thin skin that surrounded all that solidity.

He sucked in a breath. "Hold on," he said, reaching for the drawer on his nightstand. He fumbled with the foil wrapper momentarily and slipped on the condom. Within moments, he was on top of her again, skin against skin, their fast breathing in sync as his chest rose and fell against her, pressing her deeper against the sheets. He reached down and pulled one of her knees along side him.

"I've waited so long for this," he said and his hand traced up her inner thigh, into her wet opening that longed to be filled.

"Then let's not wait any longer," she murmured against his cheek as he brought his lips to hers, sliding his tongue inside her just as his cock nudged at her entrance. She took in a breath as he slid inside, stretching her slowly. Controlled. Cautious as he pushed deeper inside her, as though to take great care not to hurt her.

Deeper. His groin brushed against her clit with each thrust, making her long for the next touch.

Again. She lifted her hips upward trying to speed up his movements.

"Slowly, beautiful." He said, kissing her gently. "We don't have anyplace to go tonight." He thrust even slower, as though to make his point, and shifted slightly. And as he did, she felt his cock pressing up against her G-spot mercilessly.

"Oh, God." She inhaled as a wave of spasms shot through her body. He thrust again, shifting, and she would swear nearly killing her. But what a way to go. Heat surged out of her, searing her, sending shockwaves from her core, up her spine, across her chest, and outward so that even her fingertips were alive with sensation.

Wow. The man had obviously learned a few things about female anatomy while they'd been apart.

Her wet folds of skin seized up around him, pulling him inward, wanting more, even though her mind told her she couldn't take it. Couldn't take another thrust. Yet he did, and she came so hard she cried out, muffling her scream by pressing her mouth against his shoulder.

"Oh my God," she said breathlessly, and he only smiled knowingly in response. He pulled her onto her side, propping her knee up above his hip, and resumed the slow, seductive rhythm. As he moved inside of her, his hands ventured along her body, so warm against her skin, yet leaving a path of goose bumps in their wake.

Looking gentler now, less primal, his eyes never left hers. He looked as though he wanted to say something, yet didn't want to let any words threaten the perfection of this moment. Words were overrated, Maeve decided, seeing everything she needed to know in his eyes. He looked at her like she was beautiful. Like she was perfect. Like she was everything she was years ago and somehow even better.

She loved him for that. "I love you, Jack." Lulled by the gentle, rocking motion of his body inside of her, the words slipped from her mouth so naturally. She was only momentarily struck by the terror of regret, till he took her face in his hands and kissed her.

"I love you, too, Maeve. I always have." He said it almost casually, despite the feel of their bodies entwined, as though the three words had never been a question to him. Like she'd never again have to wonder how he felt.

She pulled him closer, and he rolled her onto her back again. Her legs wrapped around him, she locked her ankles, taking him in deeper again and he thrust, fast and hard this time, as though to possess her for eternity. Fastening her arms around his neck as he moved, she urged him to continue, to go harder, deeper, until she could finally feel him climax inside of her the way he had already felt from her.

"Faster," she said. It was only one word, and all she could manage to say feeling so breathless, so lightheaded. It felt as though that one word had cost her last ounce of breath. And he gave her what she wanted, gripping the back of her head and slamming into her till she was slick with sweat and her hair was tangled around his fingertips.

She was soaring up on a wave again, gasping for air, till finally she came just as he did, and they both cried out, until the final aftershock sank them deep into the damp sheets on his bed.

His voice was ragged as he lay on top of her. "That… was amazing."

She could barely breathe with his massive chest pinning her against the mattress. Yet she didn't want to move. "Amazing," she repeated his word, simply because her brain lacked enough oxygen to think up another.

Tracing the outline of one of his arms, her finger rose and fell among the ripples of muscle. *Perfection.*

Suddenly, nearly devoid of air, reality struck. "Can't breath, Jack. You're too big."

He swiftly moved to her side. "Sorry about that," he said with a grin. "You okay now?"

"Never better," she said, still encased in his arms. And it was every bit the truth.

PART TWO

Eight years ago

"Call me," he said, slipping a piece of paper into her hand.

He reached for her, gripping her hips, the feel of her curves in his hands arousing him as he pulled her seamlessly against him. He loved the way her body fit against his, snug and tight as she responded to his touch, urging him even closer, just as she had all weekend.

She was still in her nightgown, a simple cotton sheath with thin straps that told him she hadn't planned on inviting a man to her bed this weekend while she house-sat for her grandparents. That shouldn't have mattered to him, yet somehow it did.

Her nipples were erect against the white fabric, and he could almost make out the tempting cherry color of the buds. If only he could have another hour with her, he'd lower his mouth to them again and carry her back to bed. If only...

But it was time to go.

His number was in her hand, and even though she had told him she wouldn't call, he knew she would. There was no tossing away a connection like this. Her words about him "not fitting into her plan" would seem feeble after he walked out the door, when she remembered the moments they had shared this weekend.

He kissed her one last time—slowly at first, which took every ounce of control he had in his body. Soaking in the warmth of her breasts and belly held tight against him, he parted her lips, nearly coming undone when her tongue slipped into his mouth.

Wanting her again, right now, standing in that foyer, he realized he'd want her every day of his life.

Maeve Fischer was the real deal—something not to be taken for granted. Forever wouldn't be long enough to hold her, to talk to her, to watch her eyes light up in laughter.

He'd been around the block with plenty of women in his time at the Academy. There was something about a uniform that always kept his social calendar filled, both the days and the nights.

But this was different. This was worth exploring.

She'd call. He had no doubt about that, even as he stepped over her threshold and saw the lost look in her eyes as he shut the door behind him.

Sitting in his car, he pulled his cell phone from his pocket and set it on the seat next to him. It was a long drive to Rhode Island for Surface Warfare

Officers School. She'd call before he even made it halfway there.

Turning his key in the ignition, he smiled at the little Cape Cod, blanketed in morning sunshine. Even as his body ached to hold Maeve beneath him again, he didn't feel the slightest hint of sadness as he pulled out of the driveway.

His time with Maeve Fischer wasn't over. Not by a long shot.

CHAPTER 10

Eight years later

Impatiently, Jack checked his watch again as the morning line at Al's Donuts edged closer to the counter. It was barely 6:30, and he was hoping to be back before Maeve even awakened, though he had left a note just in case.

Chocolate frosted glazed—Jack remembered her favorite from eight years ago when he had raced here one morning during their weekend together. He hadn't known which donut she'd like the best back then, so he had gotten two dozen, one of every kind. But it had been the chocolate frosted glazed that had her mouth watering for more. Not many places actually double dip the puffy donut in a sweet glaze before spreading it with a thick coating of chocolate frosting.

He wondered if she remembered every detail, like he did. So many times in the months after he had first met Maeve, he had played the moments with her over in his mind, waiting for his cell phone to ring.

Yet it never had.

Jack wouldn't accept any back-peddling from Maeve this time, and he was fully prepared to face that battle this morning. No regrets. No "let's just be friends." So he would arrive armed—with chocolate frosted glazed donuts and a cup of coffee fixed just the way she liked it.

"Can I help you?" The girl behind the counter flashed him flirtatious smile.

I'm taken, he wanted to tell her. Completely, unequivocally spoken for. "A dozen chocolate frosted glazed. And two large coffees. Do you have some brown sugar to put in one?"

She looked at him blankly. "Brown sugar?"

"Yeah. My girlfriend likes it mixed in her coffee."

She looked only slightly downhearted at the mention of a girlfriend. "I'll go get some from the back."

Jack grinned and said his thanks, leaving an ample tip in the jar when she came back with a small scoop of brown sugar in a separate cup.

He sped home and slipped his key in the lock. He tiptoed quietly—hard to do at 6'2", 215 pounds—and peeked around the corner to his bed.

Seeing Maeve sitting there awake made him smile momentarily, till he knew the look on her face wasn't that of a satisfied lover. Had she been crying?

"I got donuts," he said cautiously.

She nodded. "I saw your note. Thanks."

"Chocolate frosted glazed, remember?"

Her pale face hinted of smile. "I remember."

In her hands she held a handful of condom wrappers, and tears were in her eyes. Unless she was crying because they had run out, this was a really bad sign.

He reached out, taking them, and tossed them into the garbage. "We were busy last night, I guess."

"Yeah."

"Maeve. You're not having regrets, are you? God, I knew you would and I'm not going to put up with it. I've got donuts and coffee for you."

She reached for the coffee.

He pulled the cup back. "But you're not getting a drop till you tell me you have no regrets." He grinned, despite the worry that gnawed at him.

"That's cruel."

"Desperate times call for desperate measures." He sat beside her, still keeping the steaming cup up out of reach. "What's going on? Talk to me. We're through holding things back now, remember?"

"Oh, Jack. It's not regret at all. God, no. More like, why the hell didn't we do this sooner?"

"I sense a 'but' coming on."

"But there is something I didn't tell you last night. I don't know how or why I didn't. I think I just got swept up in the moment."

A tear dropped, and Jack wiped it away. These past twelve hours held more emotion from Maeve than he had seen in the last two years with her smashed together. If it wasn't regret that was making her cry, what could be this bad?

Panic seized his heart, and he felt the blood rush from his face.

The cancer was back. Her fight wasn't over. *Oh God, don't let it be that. I can't lose you. I won't lose you.*

His hands were shaking—actually shaking. Disarming a missile while under enemy attack, his hands had been as still and calm as a brain surgeon's. But imagining Maeve fighting cancer was enough to make him feel completely, impossibly vulnerable. "Talk to me."

She wiped her eyes, and took a defeated breath. "I can't get pregnant."

"What?"

"I can't get pregnant. The cancer treatment— damaged my eggs."

The air rushed out of Jack's lungs. "That's *it*?"

In response, she just gazed at him, baffled.

"Christ, Maeve, you scared the hell out of me." He almost laughed—at his reaction, and at the terror he had no idea he was even capable of feeling.

"Huh?"

Relieved, he shook his head. "I thought you were going to tell me the cancer was back or something. Jesus. I need a drink." Gripping his head, he took a long sip of the coffee that still rested in his hand. "God, my hands are shaking. Look at this." He showed her, with a feeble laugh.

Maeve looked bewildered. "You don't care?"

"Of course I care. And I'm so sorry. I'm not— you know—minimizing this or something. It's just that I thought you were going to tell me something so much worse." He took her hand. "Is the cancer gone? Are you okay now?"

"According to my last check I was."

"So that's all that matters." He took her hand in his and kissed the underside of it. "Why didn't you tell me all this before? Why wait two years? I could have been some kind of support for you."

Maeve took her hand from his, scooting back onto the bed. "Hard to explain. When you looked at me, I felt like I was the same as I was at 29. There was no pity. No worry. Having you over for Scrabble, eating pizza, having barbeques—it was all like going back in time to me. You would come over nights and look at me the way you had way-back-when. You still thought I was attractive. Complete. It made me feel desired. I could tell myself that *I* was the one turning *you* down, not the other way around." She pulled the sheet around herself. "Around you, I felt I had power. I had the control. And there's something about cancer that strips a woman of control. You feel so powerless, Jack. You just don't know what it's like."

Hearing her voice trail, he moved next to her as another tear dropped just in time to kiss it away. "But you are powerful. You fought cancer and won."

"For now. But every day I'm still scared it will come back."

"And if it does, you'll fight again. And you'll be more powerful because you'll have me by your side." He took her face in her hands and kissed her. "What is it you see in my eyes now?"

Maeve shrugged.

"Any pity?"

Maeve frowned. "I guess not."

"Desire maybe?"

"Maybe."

He took her hand and led it to his already erect cock. Just sitting this close to her in bed turned him into a horny teenager. "Just maybe?" he asked playfully.

She smiled. "Maybe definitely."

"That's better. Here's your coffee. Drink up because you're gonna need your energy with me this morning." He wrapped his arm around her as she took several long, thirsty sips. "Because I haven't waited eight years to get you back in bed with me to just settle for a one-night stand." To emphasize his point, he took her coffee, set it down on the nightstand, and he gently pushed her back into the cool sheets.

"I'm open to that."

"Good." He touched his lips to hers, and wondered how someone could taste so damn good in the morning. "Because these donuts come with a price."

Maeve grinned. "So if a man buys me a donut, I'm expected to sleep with him."

"Of course. And I bought you twelve."

Pulling into her driveway, Maeve checked herself in the mirror. Her hair was disheveled, lips pink and puffy, and she was wearing the same clothes as last night.

Time to do the walk of shame.

She stepped from the car, the clicking of her heels on the concrete seeming to echo in the quiet of the late morning. She slipped her key into the lock and punched in her security code when she heard it whine after she opened the door.

"Damn well about time you came home." Lacey's eyes were narrow as she leaned against the entry to the kitchen.

Bess popped out from behind her, frowning. "I can't believe you slept with him."

Confused, Maeve's eyes darted in between the two women. They knew? "Umm. Yeah?"

"Geez, Maeve, and right after Jack's big night? You probably broke his heart if he figured it out."

Maeve cocked her head. "Okay, I'm missing something. Figured what out?"

"That you slept with Captain Shey."

Maeve laughed so hard, leaning against the wall and sliding down to the ground. "I didn't sleep with Joe. He just drove me home. Totally innocent."

Lacey raised a hand to her chest. "Oh, thank God. I just saw you leave with him, and then when you didn't come home, I assumed you were with him."

Maeve tilted her head. "Give me some credit. Though the man is as tempting as a pint of Ben and Jerry's."

Bess eyed Maeve suspiciously. "Wait a minute. You just said you slept with him. So if not Captain Shey, then… who?"

Maeve felt a blush creep up her neck. *Here we go.* No delaying the inevitable. "Jack."

Gleeful screams filled the room as Bess and Lacey grabbed each other's hands, jumping up and down like jubilant preschoolers.

Maeve rolled her eyes. "Oh, God, grow up, you two."

They continued their revelry, laughing hysterically, till they joined Maeve on the floor in an exhausted heap.

"You finished?" Maeve raised an eyebrow at her two flushed friends.

"Hey—you acted the same way when I finally slept with Mick," Lacey reminded her.

"True," Maeve admitted.

"And this was a long time coming," Bess added.

"Also true."

Bess leaned her head against the wall, grinning. "So... I'd ask how it was, but I'm guessing we already know the answer."

"It was... he was..." Trying to put it into words was impossible for Maeve. "God, he's amazing."

"So, I take it you told him everything."

"Everything. No more secrets."

Bess's eyes hinted of relief. "And see? It didn't bother him at all, did it?"

Maeve shrugged. "He says he doesn't care. I mean, we're just taking it one day at a time, you know? I'll never marry him, but—"

"What?" Lacey lifted a hand. "Wait a second. Why?"

Maeve lowered her chin. "Well, for one thing, we just started this. Marriage isn't nearly in the picture. And it's stupid to wonder how or when it will end when we just began." She stood up, brushing off her wrinkled dress. "All this time, we could have been enjoying time together, and I wouldn't go there because I knew it would only end. So what? Most the relationships we start in life end miserably. But does that mean we don't enjoy the ride?"

Lacey and Bess exchanged a look.

Bess stood. "Guess you're right. But I still wouldn't count on ending it, Maeve."

"Believe me, I am counting on it. He deserves more. Hell, I deserve more."

"Huh." Lacey looked unconvinced.

"But that doesn't mean we can't enjoy each other until this thing burns itself out. He's only going to be here another few weeks anyway."

"Mm'kay." Lacey said, glancing at Bess. "She's not much of a romantic, is she?"

"So when are you seeing him next?" Bess asked, offering her hand to Lacey and giving her a tug.

"Tonight. He said since he's leaving soon, he wants to spend as much time with me as possible."

Bess followed Maeve toward the kitchen. "Aww. Where are you going?"

"I'm hoping nowhere. I haven't had sex that good in years, and I can't get more of that in public." Maeve sighed. "Why the hell didn't I do this sooner?"

"I have no idea."

Maeve sat at the table. "And how am I going to live without it when he leaves?"

Lacey smiled. "As Mick always says, 'We'll base jump off that bridge when we come to it.'"

"Come on. I'm making omelets to celebrate."

Maeve laughed. "Wow. You know it's been a long time since you've gotten laid when your friends want to celebrate with you after."

"That's not all we're celebrating." Standing at the refrigerator, Bess glanced over her shoulder. "I checked your blog yesterday and you got 36 comments last week."

"You're sure they're not just my mom and dad posting under false names?"

"Positive they're not. Some were even from out of the country. Italy, Spain. There was even one from Hawaii."

"Hawaii's not another country, Bess."

Bess gave her a look. "I know that. But my point is, word is spreading. Jack's military angle was brilliant. They're sharing your posts on Facebook, too."

"And you're doing such a good thing," Lacey added. Sitting beside her, she opened her laptop. "All the comments are so positive. Everyone is saying thank you and how hard it is to make a house feel like a home after moving so much. That entry you wrote about the girl's room was fabulous, and all those links you put in there."

Maeve grinned, looking at her blog on Lacey's computer. "Now if I can just get a paying client out of it."

"You will." She shut her laptop. "Now don't get too settled. You need to get ready before eating." Lacey looked at her closely. "You look a little… umm… unkempt."

Bess scoffed. "That's one word for it."

"Amazing sex does that to me. But what's the rush? I want my omelet."

"We're leaving for Edith's soon. Bridal shower. Remember?"

"Oh my God. I forgot!"

"Yeah, and she's invited all her rich old friends so that Lacey can get some good gifts. So wearing yesterday's clothes and smelling like—" she cleared her throat, "—well, anyway. Just shower. Okay?"

"Give me a half hour. Don't put my omelet on yet, okay?"

Bess gave her a once-over. "We'll give you an hour. For once, you need it."

CHAPTER 11

Jack rolled over on the bed and reached for his watch.

"What are you doing?" Maeve asked, snuggled into his blankets and reaching for him.

"I've got to set my alarm for tomorrow. I get up at 4:30 for PT." After a few beeps, he set it back down. "Tell me that won't stop you from spending the night. You can just roll over and go back to sleep."

Maeve groaned. Having a body like his had a price, but she hadn't considered she might have to pay for it, too. "4:30? You get up at 4:30 to exercise?"

"'Fraid so."

"Okay. Waking up at 4:30 is a bit of a price to pay. You're going to have to make it worth my while the night before."

"Believe me. I plan to."

He slid on top of her body and the warmth of him penetrated her skin. She kicked the blanket away. Jack was a much more enjoyable heat source.

"This weekend has been the best I've ever had in Annapolis," he said with a grin.

"Better than eight years ago?"

"Hard to believe we could top that, but yes, even better." His voice was muffled as he dotted a string of kisses from her chin down to her naval.

Curious, she tilted her head to one side. "So, where were your better weekends?"

"Huh?"

"You said this was your best weekend in Annapolis specifically. So, where were the better ones?"

Pulling his head up from her belly, Jack laughed. "Nothing gets by you, does it?" He lay back, looking thoughtful for a moment.

"Well?"

"I'm still thinking." He pressed lips together, gazing up at the ceiling fan with determination. "Nope. Can't think of any other weekends anywhere to top it."

"And it took you that long to figure it out?"

He smiled, angling his body over hers, and kissed her neck. "When I say something, I want to make sure it's the truth. I'll never lie to you." He lifted the t-shirt she was wearing over her head. "How about you?"

"Me?" Her voice went up a pitch as he took her nipple in his mouth.

"What better weekends have you had?" He cupped a breast in both his hands and suckled gently.

"No fair," she said, her temperature rising. "How am I supposed to think when you're doing that?"

"I have to use what I have to my advantage." He moved to her left breast with his mouth while his hand kneaded the right one.

"Mmmm…" Maeve could feel herself growing wet and weak. "When Abigail was born," she finally offered. "Remember how Bess had been in the hospital a few weeks before that? I don't think I slept a full night till she was born. And then, there she was, and I felt this relief that I can't even put into words."

Jack dropped his chin on top of her belly and raised his eyebrows. "I got beat out by Abigail's birth?"

"Kind of, but," she began as he resumed a downward path of kisses, "it was a completely different kind of wonderful." Her voice became low and breathless when his mouth met her mound. "Oh, God. Yes, it was completely different." She struggled to keep talking as he toyed with her. "I had just never experienced that before. You have all your nieces and nephews. I don't. My brother won't ever have kids."

He looked up at her. "Why not?"

"He says they make too much of a mess. Too much drool and dribble and noise and smells."

"Sounds like some of the lines I've been hearing from you for two years."

"I probably stole one or two from him. Yeah." She stroked his hair as she pressed him closer. "Sorry I lied to you about all that."

He didn't answer for a moment, paying too much attention to one particularly responsive square inch on her body. Then he smiled. "I accept your apology, so long as you'll never lie to me again."

"Promise." She gasped, and his fingers entered her. "Especially if you keep doing things like that."

"If it makes you feel better," he started, moving his fingers in and out of her body, "you never fooled me for a moment. At least, not since Abby was born."

"Mmmm." She murmured, unable to come up with words.

He eased back up her, gently resting his hand on her stomach. "I'll get a key made for you tomorrow so you can come and go as you please."

"You don't need to get me a key. You're leaving so soon anyway." Even saying the words seemed to burn her heart. Either that, or it was General Tso chicken they had eaten a couple hours ago.

"Yeah, but I want every minute I can with you, Maeve." He wound a lock of her hair around one of his fingers and let it go, seeming entranced by the way it fell onto the pillow. "It's commissioning week. Tons to do, but I'd really like you by my side for as much as you can."

"I'm unemployed, remember? I think I can fit you in."

"Good. At least there are some benefits to being unemployed."

His hand dropped to her waist, kneading the skin gently, which seemed to urge her to move her own body flush against his. She turned to her side, resting her leg on him.

He pulled her even closer. "Tomorrow I've got a couple division award ceremonies I need to attend. Pretty boring stuff. But at 1:30 they're doing the Herndon climb. Want to go?"

"What's the Herndon Climb?"

"Each year, they grease up the Herndon monument and the mids team up to try to climb it."

Maeve raised an eyebrow. "And they do this *why* exactly?"

"To put an officer's cover on top of it."

"Cover?"

"A hat, Maeve. A cover is a hat. Geez, I've got to help you get up on these terms. How long have you lived in Annapolis?"

Maeve lightly smacked him with a pillow. "So, they climb a greased up monument to put a hat on it? And these are the men who will be defending our country?"

"It's symbolic for the end of their time as plebes. Tradition. It's fun, Maeve. Lighten up. They go through a lot of stress for four years."

Maeve smiled. "I know, I know. I can't resist giving you a hard time though."

"So you want to go?"

"Of course. How can a girl resist the invitation to watch a bunch of young fit men get greasy and climb on top of each other? I'll bring my camera."

"I knew that would appeal." He took her hand and moved it to his arousal, shutting his eyes gratefully as she gripped him. "There's a concert nearly every day this week. I'll get you a schedule and if there are any you'd like to go to, I'll take you."

"Thanks." She stroked him, hard, wondering what she would have to do to finally get him to stop talking. His genius brain was always working, able to do ten things at once. She wanted to push him as far as she could.

He grinned at the pressure of her hand on him. "Then the Blue Angels do their air show on Wednesday if you're up for it."

She stopped. "God, yes! I've never actually seen it downtown, but even from my neighborhood I see them flying overhead. I've always wanted to see it up close."

"Best way to see it is on a boat. And I might be able to arrange for that." He moved his hand toward hers, urging her to continue.

"Don't fill our schedule too much. We still have a wedding to plan for."

"We'll get it done..." his voice trailed momentarily, his erection thrumming in her hand. "And I get a plus one for the graduation if you want to go."

"What's a plus one?"

"A date. Me, plus one. Don't civilians say that, too?"

More determined, she lowered herself down his body. "I've never heard that term before. But I don't get around much."

"Yeah, right." As her lips met his cock, he sucked in a breath. But he seemed to know the game she was playing with him, even as she took him deep in her mouth. "It's pretty damn—" He let out a moan. "—incredible to see. The graduation. The President will be there. Oh. My. God."

She barely lifted her mouth from him to say, "That good, huh? The graduation, I mean." She dropped her mouth onto him again eagerly, glancing upward to see his eyes slam shut.

His fingers rammed into her shoulders suddenly, lifting her off of him, tossing her on her stomach. "I won't last another minute if you keep that up." He reached for a condom. "Shit. We're out."

His body was behind her, his cock pressing into her back as he shook the empty box just to be certain.

"Jack, I can't get pregnant. And I had myself tested last time I went in for my cancer screening. I haven't been with anyone since then."

"They just tested me at my physical two weeks ago. I could even show you the paperwork, if you want."

She laughed. "That's the first time I've heard that one." She reached behind her, urging him to press harder against her backside. "So why not just…?" She didn't complete the sentence. Just gave a little shrug in lieu of words.

"You're sure?" he asked, reaching around her to find her moist and ready.

"God, yes."

He bent her at the knees, and moved his hand to her opening, toying a moment, spreading the moisture around the delicate folds. From behind, he slid inside her, moving gently and reaching around her to play with her nub that begged to be touched. He licked his fingers, and then brought that moisture to her clit, circling it over and over as he thrust into her depths.

Wanting more, she rose up onto her knees, her forearms in the pillow. He was still inside of her, stroking her clit gently between two fingers. "Does that feel good, baby?"

Her mind swirling, she couldn't even manage a reply. She wanted more, so much more. *Read my mind, Jack.*

He rose up behind her, thrusting harder, his hands moving up to her breasts, massaging them. Then, grabbing her butt as he thrust, he squeezed the flesh so hard she cried out. But the only word she could utter was, "Yes."

There was something erotic about his body behind her, unable to see his powerful muscles as he took her, only able to focus on the granite-hard erection driving inside of her. Deeper and deeper he took her, reaching her innermost depths, causing her to scream into the pillow as she came, every nerve on her body writhing, aching, and yet still wanting more.

He slowed his thrusts as the last quake shook her. She was pliant now, boneless, enabling him to move her legs around, lifting one across his chest, until he could face her, with him still hard inside of her.

"Jack," she said, as her eyes drank him in. It was as though she was just remembering how perfect every feature on his body was. His shoulders, with thick vessels now pulsating against his taut muscles. Her eyes were drawn to his abs that led a rippled path down him to the point where they were joined. She gazed at the image a moment, almost feeling it was surreal— this man, completely consumed by her. He pulled out slowly to his tip, and stopped, and she watched, entranced, as he slid back inside. Free of a condom, he was silky and rigid. Long and thick.

"You like to watch," he observed.

She didn't answer, only reached for the exposed part of his cock and traced a finger along it as he slipped inside her again.

"Oh, baby."

He kept his back arched, his torso far enough from her that she could get a full view as he did it again, allowing her to feel his erection slide out and then back in, as she pressed a finger against him.

"I can't hold on much longer," he said, quickening his rhythm as she pulled him closer.

"Then don't," she whispered as he kissed her, urging her mouth open with his lips till she could taste him. And still she wanted more.

Her hands moved to his back, feeling the muscles tighten and release as he moved his body. Her breath quickened, matching his, and she watched his eyelids drop, as though he was savoring the sensation of her body beneath him.

This was heaven, she thought, as her body responded intuitively to every touch, every thrust, every sensation. Her mind had lost control, and instinct had taken over, hips rising and falling, back arching, heart slamming.

The feel of him inside her was so wild and addictive, she knew she would never be the same.

Giving in, she climbed to a peak of pleasure. And she came undone, crying out his name only moments before he spilled himself inside of her with a final thrust. She nearly wept from the feel of him seeping into her, warm and deep. Another string of spasms took her by surprise, as though her body were taking every ounce of him inside her, unwilling to let go.

"Oh..." she moaned. Low and thick, she could barely recognize her own voice.

He gently moved her to her side, still inside of her. "Maeve." He said her name possessively, reverently.

A satisfied smile crept up her face, and it took a moment before she could form words. Finally, she was able to murmur, "Come to think of it, I think that weekend Abigail was born is really a close second."

CHAPTER 12

Maeve touched the "end" button on her phone. Her heart was racing.

A client. A *paying* client who had seen Maeve's work online and was interested in turning his basement into a crafting room for his wife. She had stuck with him thirty years while he was in the Navy. And now that he had retired, he wanted to give her something nice.

"The sky's the limit," he had said. Four words every designer longs to hear.

She set her phone down on the kitchen table and raced toward Abigail's room. Lacey was at Mick's, but Bess was home. "Bess?" she said quietly, her head next to the baby's closed door.

"Hold your breath if you come in here, Maeve."

Even the mild threat couldn't keep Maeve from sharing her news with someone face-to-face. She swung open the door. "I've got my first— ugh!" Instinctively, she stepped backward as she hit a wall of stench. "Good God. What did you feed her last night?"

Her face curled in revulsion, Bess wiped Abigail's messy bottom. "I tried making apricot baby food with that Vitamix someone gave Lacey at the bridal shower. I had no idea the homemade stuff would have this kind of effect on her. She eats the kind from the store all the time without… this," she finished, glancing downward to the mess.

"Phew, Abigail." Maeve eyed the baby as she took another step back. "You sure know how to clear a room."

"So, what's so important that you'd dare come into the danger zone?"

Maeve grinned. "I've got my first client."

"No! Really?" She beamed. "That's great! I'd hug you, but I'm germy now."

"Yeah. Keep your hands to yourself. And I shouldn't even say anything yet, because we've just talked on the phone. I'm going to meet with him this afternoon. But he really liked what he saw on my website. Or *your* website, I should say."

"It's your work on there that makes the site good. I just put it all together." She tossed a final dirty wipe into the trashcan. "How did he find out about you?"

"He's in the Navy. Or was, till a few weeks ago. Someone forwarded him a link to my blog."

"Brilliant. Jack's idea is working." She slipped a fresh diaper under Abby. "Did you tell Jack yet?"

"No. I want to tell him in person."

"So you can thank him properly?"

Maeve blushed. "Sort of like that."

Bess lifted Abigail and started toward her crib.

"I'll hold her," Maeve offered, taking the warm baby into her arms. She hadn't experienced any better feeling in the world than having Abigail nestled against her... until recently. Being held in Jack's arms definitely had taken the lead.

"Oh, sure. *Now* you offer. Where was your help when she smelled like a septic tank exploded?" Bess laughed, as she opened the door to the bathroom, scoured her hands, and wiped down the doorknob she had touched with a Lysol wipe.

Maeve didn't know whether it came from motherhood or cleaning people's houses for a living, but her friend could easily work as a cross-contamination expert for the Centers for Disease Control.

"So how are you two doing, anyway?" Bess reached for Abigail. "You've barely been around the house these days. Always at his place."

"We're—wonderful." Maeve leaned against the wall. "We're still in that stage where we can't get enough of each other. He's been so busy winding up the school year and getting things ready for his move. So we're just fitting in time together whenever we can. He took me to the Herndon Climb yesterday—you know, when all the mids climb up this greased up obelisk? You should totally go next year, Bess. They're too young for me to even look at without feeling like a cougar-in-training. But if I were 23 like you, I'd be standing there handing out my number."

Bess laughed. "A man is the last thing I need."

"And the first thing you need is—?"

"Eight hours of uninterrupted sleep."

"Okay, okay." Maeve lifted her hands. "Just a suggestion."

"Are you seeing him today?"

"Yeah. There's a pipes and drums concert tonight in the rotunda. You should come. I bet Abby would love the music."

"Nah. I've got some studying to do."

"But you're still coming to the Blue Angels flight demonstration, right?"

Bess shook her head. "Sounds like too much noise and heat for Abby. Besides, if we'd really be seeing it from a boat, I just wouldn't feel comfortable with a baby, you know?"

"So, we'll ask Edith if she'll babysit."

"No. Really, I'm fine with it."

"Not acceptable. You need a life, Bess. When was the last time you got out and did something different?"

Bess lowered Abby into her crib. "I need a life. I won't argue with that. But what you need is time alone with Jack. He won't be around here much longer. I have no intentions of being the third wheel."

Maeve crossed her arms. "We're all going. I'm calling Edith now."

"No, you're not. I can be just as stubborn as you. I'll go next year."

"Next year Jack and Mick will be gone." She hated even speaking those words.

"So? I'll go with the hot mid I'll pick up at the Herndon climb," Bess said with a smile.

Maeve grinned. "Now you're talking."

"Now go. You have your first client meeting to get ready for."

"I've always wanted to go here," Maeve admitted as Jack pulled the chair out for her at their table overlooking the Bay. He had insisted on taking her out that night to Eagle's Point after the concert to celebrate her first client.

"This is Lacey and Mick's place, isn't it?" Jack took her hand as he sat down.

"Mmhm. She says they kind of fell in love here, I guess."

"With this view, it's hard not to." Jack's eyes never left hers.

Maeve glanced out the window, and soaked in the sweeping sight of the Bay in the moonlight. "So true."

"I meant you. The view of you, not the water."

If any other man had said such a thing, she would have called it a line. But not with Jack.

"This can't be our place, though," he said casually, glancing down at his menu. "I'm already in love with you."

Maeve played along. "So what is our place? Where did you fall for me?"

Jack's smile was filled with a wealth of memories. "Easy. Your back porch. Playing Scrabble. Eating burgers that Mick had overcooked on the barbeque."

Maeve scrunched up her face. "He really does lack talent with a Weber, doesn't he? We've eaten so much better since Bess took over the cooking."

It was to be a late dinner, and Maeve couldn't help recall her days of living in New York City while she was in design school, where it was practically a city law to never eat dinner before eight.

Her life was so different now in Annapolis, a sleepy little town by comparison, she thought, glancing over the wine list. No cheap wines here, she noted, but Jack had refused to take her anyplace else.

A little indulgence would do her good, and with the timer ticking away, she wouldn't get too many opportunities to enjoy an elegant meal with Jack. Yet still...

"You really didn't have to take me out, Jack. In fact, I should be the one taking you out, seeing as the only reason I got a client is because of you."

"Don't be ridiculous. Besides, it's nice to get you out doing something that isn't at the Academy for a change. Did you like the concert?"

"Yes. I've never heard bagpipes performed live before. They sound so eerie and beautiful. Gave me chills." Spotting what she wanted on the menu, she closed it and set it down in front of her. "And everything always sounds even better when it's at the Academy. There's something about those historic buildings that just lend such meaning to everything."

"I know. It was hard going to school there because of it. So much pressure, feeling the weight of centuries of tradition on your shoulders."

"So, is that how your shoulders got that strong?"

"That, and a lot of overhead presses at the gym."

They ordered appetizers and wine, and Maeve's mouth watered at their arrival. There was no dieting in this place, to be sure. But she now had a marvelous way of working off every wicked calorie.

"So I haven't overbooked you, have I?" Jack asked. "I think I've got you busy every day this week."

"I'm loving it. I've never experienced commencement week this way before. Till now, it had always been a week I dreaded. You know, all the traffic."

Jack smiled. "It's a little different on the other side of the Academy gates, isn't it?" he reached for her hand as the waitress approached.

He ordered their entrées, as he always did. He might be a Northerner, but he had more Southern charm than half the population of Charleston. She'd love to take him there one day, have him meet her mother.

Oh no. She gave herself a shake, wiping the idea from her head. Jack was not hers for keeping. Just hers for enjoying right now.

"Are you cold?" he asked. "You gave a little shudder there." He stood, pulling off his suit jacket and putting it on her shoulders.

"Thanks," she said, unable to turn down the sweet gesture even though she wasn't cold. She smiled at the sight of him in a shirt and tie. They fit him impeccably, not too tight, not too loose.

Yet still his muscles revealed their size beneath the cotton blend.

"What?"

He must have noticed her grinning at him. "I just have never seen you in a suit," she said. "A real suit. I mean—civilian. You're always dressed casually or in your uniform."

He cocked his head. "And does the sight please you, milady?" he asked playfully, brushing his lips against her hand.

"Yes. Yes, it definitely does." Something about seeing him this way made her picture it— him headed in to a normal office job in DC or Baltimore. Cup of Starbucks in the car with him as he sliced his way through rush hour traffic. Kissing goodbye the life of risk and upheaval that comes with being in the military. And coming home to… someone other than herself, of course.

Someone damned lucky.

Yet still, a man like Jack wouldn't be content living his life in a normal nine to five job. Pushing papers. Whittling down the pile in his "in" box to only see it stack up again.

Jack was meant for the military. Same way as his dad was, Maeve imagined.

"How many years was your dad in the Marines?" she asked, and took a sip of her wine.

"The full thirty."

"Thirty? I thought it was twenty years till retirement."

"Twenty till officers can retire with benefits. But you can stay in until thirty. Then, you're out—unless they promote you to Admiral. Or General in my dad's case, since he was a Marine.

But he left as a full Colonel, and that's something to be proud of, I think."

"God, yes," Maeve agreed. "So… an Admiral, huh? Is that what you want to be when you hit thirty?"

Seeing her empty glass, he poured her more wine. "At this point, at thirty years I just want to be alive." His eyes flew up to hers, as though he knew how she would react. "Sorry. Didn't mean it like that. It's just been a long war, you know?"

"Yeah." She did know. Knew better than she had only days ago. Something about spending so much time on base this week, meeting other officers like Jack and talking to their families, made her see first-hand how long the war had been.

"Most of my jobs are pretty dull," he assured her. "Not risk-free, but I think sometimes the commute into DC can be riskier."

Maeve nodded, relieved to hear his words. "You're not kidding. I wasn't looking forward to the possibility of getting a job in there. Highway 50's even worse than I-97 in the morning."

"But now you don't have to." Jack raised his glass. "We really should toast. To Maeve Fisher Designs, Annapolis's latest successful business."

She raised her own. "And to the man who put it on the map." She sipped as she took his other hand, wondering how she'd ever let it go.

CHAPTER 13

With the window open, Bess could hear the gentle laughter of her friends coming from the back porch. Sliding a fresh diaper underneath Abigail, she smiled. Things were exactly as they were meant to be. Lacey and Mick. Maeve and Jack.

She frowned momentarily, glancing out the window. "The cheese stands alone."

A little coo from Abby snapped her eyes back to her precious child. "Not with you in my life, I'm not alone." She lifted her, cradling her, savoring the feel of Abby's soft skin against her, and breathing in her scent as though it brought her strength.

Because it did. It really did.

She laid her down in her crib and turned on the mobile. Stepping back, she watched Abby's eyes transfixed on the little fairies as they traveled in a circle around her head.

They'd be okay. She'd make sure of that. Thanks to Maeve, she had saved up enough money for a nice apartment and she was only weeks away from getting her degree. But God, she'd miss this place if Maeve decided to leave Annapolis to be with Jack. Maeve hadn't mentioned anything about it, but Bess thought she better prepare herself for the inevitable.

It made her happy, really it did, she convinced herself as she walked into the kitchen and grabbed a brownie from the counter. Heck, she had practically pushed the two of them together these past weeks. They were meant to be together. Just like Lacey and Mick.

And Bess and… Abigail. She nodded a little to herself. They were a team, the two of them. She didn't need anyone else.

Leaning against the counter, she looked at Lacey's luggage, already packed and leaning against the wall by the garage door. Tomorrow she and Mick would be flying out to San Diego for a couple days to look at houses. Lacey was so eager to take this next step in their relationship.

Houses. She shook her head, trying to imagine Lacey living anywhere but here.

It had only been two years that she'd lived here with her friends. Yet it seemed so much longer. Her life had been split into two chapters. Before Annapolis. And after.

The after was so much better than the before.

Opening the back door, she was comforted by the sight of her friends around the table, just as they had been so many times before. This might be the last time she'd see them this way, drinking their beers and playing Scrabble like a bunch of board game addicts.

"Abigail asleep?" Maeve glanced up from her tiles.

"Probably will be in about two seconds." Bess sat beside her.

"Don't get chocolate on the tiles, Bess. We'll end up with ants in the closet again." Maeve frowned. "Not to be critical, but isn't that your third one?"

"Yeah. I don't know what's wrong with me these days." Of course, she knew what was wrong. For her, anxiety was a monster that demanded to be fed. And watching everyone in her household go separate ways was more difficult than she'd ever admit to her friends.

Mick reached for a handful of nachos. "It's boredom. You're 23. You should be out tonight rather than hanging out with a bunch of thirty-something cronies like us." He crunched on a chip. "Jack and I need to find you a nice ensign."

Lacey smiled knowingly. "I think if Bess were to fall for someone in uniform it would be an Army guy."

Mick and Jack glanced at each other.

"Not that cadet. Taylor." Jack said his name with a disdain.

"Tyler," Bess corrected. "And he's not a cadet anymore. He's a Ranger-qualified second lieutenant," she added, a hint of pride in her voice.

Mick narrowed his eyes. "I don't like him. Sends too much West Point propaganda."

"They're Army t-shirts and onesies for Abby, Mick. Not propaganda."

"And there was that West Point cheerleader outfit. What one-year-old has one of those?" Jack took a sip of his beer. "Obviously he's trying to recruit Abigail. And if she's going to put on any uniform when she grows up, it'll be Navy. It's far more cerebral."

Mick tilted his head in Jack's direction. "I get shot at too much to call the Navy cerebral."

"We're just friends, guys," Bess interrupted. "He's still got a girlfriend. One who is about six sizes smaller than me who doesn't have a butt that cascades halfway down her thighs."

"Your butt doesn't cascade anywhere," Maeve defended. "And you had a baby. Cut yourself some slack."

"I had a baby a year ago. And I weigh as much now as I did when I was six months along."

Jack snatched the other half of the brownie that Bess had just set down on a napkin. "You look fine. And these are damn good brownies you made. Worth every fat cell."

"Says the guy who works out daily," Bess tossed at him.

"So? Come running with me one day. We'll get you one of those jogging strollers. Maeve, you in? We can make it a morning thing."

Maeve smiled slyly. "If I wake up before dawn with you, there's something I'd much rather do than go jogging." She leaned in and gave him a sultry kiss.

Bess rolled her eyes. It was her only defense. "So first I had to put up with Lacey and Mick, and now I have to survive you and Jack? I'm a haggard, undersexed mom trapped in a house with two blissfully happy couples. My life is so depressing."

Jack's lips were still a breath away from Maeve's, as he glanced at Bess. "Sorry, kid.

You're on your own running. But I wouldn't sweat it. I don't understand why women obsess so much about looking perfect." He kissed Maeve again briefly before settling back into his chair. "A guy goes blind out of gratitude if he gets you to bed, anyway."

Maeve laughed. "Is that how it is?"

"Hell, yeah. Right, Mick?"

"Yup. Lacey could have a tattoo of Howard Stern on her chest and I wouldn't even know it."

Bess smiled. As crude as they could be, Jack and Mick always had a way of making her feel better. They were like the big brothers she never had, and always wanted. "It doesn't matter anyway. I don't date. I'm a mom, remember?"

Maeve's eyes didn't leave her tiles as she shifted them around, looking for inspiration. "So what? Hey—how about that guy who came to give an estimate for spraying our yard for mosquitoes? I saw you drooling out the window after he left."

Bess sighed. "Yeah. Call me crazy, but there's nothing sexier than a man who's that cute and rids our yard of mosquitoes. When he pulled up in his big black truck I thought I heard angels sing."

Jack snorted. "There have been stranger attractions, I'm sure."

Bess wiped a trace of frosting from her hands with a napkin and put three tiles on the board. "Nothing strange about it. You haven't seen how those bugs come after Abigail. The man is my hero."

Maeve jotted down Bess's score. "Well, he'll be coming back two days before the wedding to spray. It's either that, or hand out bug repellent for the party favors." She plunked down a few tiles. "Read it and weep."

"Ouch. Another triple word score for Maeve," Lacey said, finishing off her glass of Chardonnay. "Speaking of party favors. Any ideas? 'Cause I'm clueless."

"Shouldn't it be something to go along with the theme?" Bess asked.

"And our theme is… what? I hadn't really thought about it." Lacey's eyes darted back and forth among her friends.

Jack's shoulders sagged. "We need a theme?"

Maeve tilted her head. "You want a theme? Here it is: shotgun wedding. Because if we manage to pull this off with less than two weeks left, it will definitely qualify."

"Not shotgun. It's a SEAL wedding. It should be an HK416," Mick suggested.

"Lovely. An HK416 themed wedding. How romantic." Maeve took a sip of her Fresca, having already hit her limit on wine that evening. "We'll give out little tea lights shaped like machine guns. Perfect."

"The guys would love it."

"Seriously, though," Maeve began, stretching her arms out to the Bay. "That's our theme. Waterfront. The Bay. Navy. With a view like that and a bunch of hot SEALs swarming the scene, that's all the theme we need."

"Hot SEALs?" Jack pulled her neck closer possessively and planted a kiss on her lips so hot it actually made Bess feel a pang of jealousy. "I better remind you who you are going home with that night."

"I don't need a reminder." Maeve grinned. "Oh, hey—how about this? We're doing a candy bar, right? So we could get some glass jars engraved with Lacey and Mick's names on them, and guests can fill them with candy. Maybe have a little wave design or a sailboat or skyline of Annapolis on them. Something like that."

"Engraved? You're dreaming. We'd never get that in time."

Mick leaned forward. "I have an idea."

Maeve eyed him suspiciously. "Yeah, sure. Not up for one of your jokes now. We need to be serious about this."

"I *am* serious. I have an idea. We could probably get nice looking mason jars and wrap them in some kind of adhesive label with guests' names on them and the wedding date on it. Print them out on my color printer. That won't take any time at all. We can even put them out on the tables and they can double as place cards. Then guests can fill them with candy at the candy bar."

Maeve looked at him blankly.

Mick's brow furrowed. "What? Don't you like the idea?"

Maeve's eyes widened. "I think it's great. But I just can't believe a SEAL with a six-pack and a Navy Cross knows what a mason jar is."

Lacey snorted. "They're really trendy in weddings right now. And I've made him watch at least twenty hours of those wedding shows on TLC."

Jack raised his bottle in Mick's direction. "That's taking one for the team, my brother."

"No shit."

"Quarter!" Bess called out with enthusiasm. Maeve had put an empty jug out on the kitchen counter labeled "Bad word jar" that night, and anyone who said something foul had to make a 25-cent offering toward Abby's college fund. At the rate her friends were swearing tonight, she'd have a year at NYU covered by the end of summer.

"Again?" Mick grumbled.

Maeve glared. "Hey, I had to do something to clean up the language around here. Abby's due to say her first word any day now, and I don't want her talking like a sailor, even though she is surrounded by them. Now pay up."

Mick reluctantly rose, reaching into his pocket. "I'm going to go broke around here." He stopped in the doorway and turned. "So what do you think? We can buy some jars this weekend, put on the labels, and we'll be GTG."

Maeve raised her eyebrows. "GTG?"

"Good to go," Mick and Jack responded in unison.

"I really need to brush up on my acronyms to survive around you guys." Bess handed Mick Lacey's wine glass. "Lacey needs a refill while you are in there, Mick."

"No, I don't," Lacey protested.

"Actually—" Bess began with a sigh, "—you do. And get yourself another beer while you're at it, Mick," she called toward the door.

Lacey looked concerned. "What's going on?"

"Well," she began, pausing until Mick had returned, drinks in hand. "I've been dreading telling you this, but I got an email from the caterer. Seems they double-booked us with a bar mitzvah. And the bar mitzvah won. She says they don't have enough staff to cover two events."

"What do you mean?" Lacey's face paled.

"We have no caterer."

Maeve's eyes bugged out. "And you've been sitting on this information all night?"

"I thought they'd take it better after a couple drinks," Bess told her.

"Probably smart there," Maeve said under her breath.

Bess could swear she saw steam rising from Mick's head. "We've got 110 people showing up in two weeks. 30 of them are hungry SEALs. What are we going to feed them?"

"Raw fish?" Maeve offered, and Bess suppressed a snort of laughter, seeing the lethal look Mick shot her in response. Maeve shrunk in her seat. "Sorry, hon. You walked right into that one. I couldn't resist."

Lacey's eyes were filled with panic. "Can they do that? I mean, we have a contract. We should call a lawyer."

"And that would gain us what? A mountain of lawyer's fees? I think the best thing we can do is just give them a really shitty review online." Grumbling another curse, Mick stood up.

"Where are you going?" Bess asked.

"I'm putting a twenty in the quarter jar—for all the words that I'm about to say,"

"Well, keep your twenty for a minute longer, because I have an idea." Bess bit her lip. "How about I do the cooking?"

Mick dropped back down into his chair, and the room fell silent.

Lacey's mouth hung open a bit. "There will be, like 110 people, maybe."

"I can do it. Think about it. We had 22 people over last Thanksgiving and I didn't even break a sweat. Most of the stuff I can make ahead of time. I could make my cream of crab you guys like so much for the soup. Maybe a Maryland style for a second option. We could have a few carving stations for meat. A couple hams and roast beefs. Then we do a mashed potato bar."

"Like the one we saw on that wedding show we watched yesterday?" Maeve interrupted.

"Exactly. People love them. And I'd make that asparagus and wild rice dish you like, Lacey. Green beans in garlic sauce. Or maybe a couple Hawaiian dishes to sort of pull in your honeymoon destination into the menu." Bess could feel a warmth cast over her skin. It was almost weird how excited she got over cooking. "I wouldn't even have to do the appetizers. We can order some of those mini-crab cakes from Jesse's Fish House, and maybe a giant kettle of crab dip and bread. It's very Annapolis, don't you think? All I'd have to do is heat them up. Then we'd have cocktail shrimp and plenty of it. Cheese and fruit plate. There's nothing to that. You just serve it."

"Yeah, but *who*? Who serves it? We were counting on the caterer for that."

"I already checked with the same place who we hired to bartend. They can do it. They'll set up, serve, and even clean up."

Maeve raised her eyebrows at Lacey.

Lacey shook her head. "Bess, it's so sweet to offer this. But I'm not letting you cook at my wedding. You're my bridesmaid. Not my cook."

"I'd love it. Cooking is what makes me happy. You know that. If I could pull this off..." Her voice trailed a moment, lost in a dream.

"That's a lot of food to prepare."

Bess leaned forward, moving in for the kill. "We've got five ovens among us. Yours, Mick's, Jack's, and I already talked to Edith about using her double oven. She even told me she has an extra refrigerator in her basement. And the company we're renting chairs from also rents restaurant equipment, like serving platters and huge chafing dishes."

"You've done your homework. When did you get this news?" Jack asked.

"Yesterday. But I didn't want to tell you till I had a plan. Figured one more day wouldn't make a difference."

"And you're sure you want to take this on?"

"More than anything. I need this. God, I need to know I can successfully do something other than change a diaper or clean a toilet."

Jack exchanged a look with Mick. "We could do it on the cheap if Mick and I bought the groceries at the commissary."

Maeve interjected. "Yeah, the one perk to the military. Sure, they shoot at your husband, but you get cheap groceries out of the deal."

Bess scooted her chair closer to Lacey's, seeing a new angle to sell this to her. Lacey was notoriously practical when it came to money. "They're right. Even with the rental equipment and staff, we'd come in way under budget. Much less than that stupid caterer and it would be twice as good, if I do say so myself." She grinned slyly. "You'd have a lot more money for your down payment. Or maybe extra cash to furnish your house. Imagine all you could buy at Pottery Barn."

Lacey bit her lip, and Bess could swear she saw visions of new loveseats, coffee tables, and headboards dancing in her friend's eyes.

"You're sure?" Lacey asked in a tentative voice. "I mean, Bess, you've got so much going on right now with school ending. And you've got a baby, for God's sake."

"Maeve and I volunteer to babysit while she's cooking," Jack offered, clasping Maeve's hand and raising it with his own.

Bess touched Lacey's arm hesitantly, feeling almost desperate for her to say yes. Playing caterer for the day sounded more fun to her than she'd had in her lifetime. "I really want this. I want to do something for you for a change. All of you are always doing things for me. Finally I feel like I have something to offer."

"Yeah, Bess, you only cook a gourmet meal for us twice a week. Come on," Mick responded.

She glanced his way briefly. "Sure, with food that you guys buy for me, and in a kitchen that's not my own. So what?"

"For a guy who eats cold Chinese take-out on nights I'm not here, it seems like plenty," Jack said.

Bess folded her arms. "Well, Chinese take-out is the next alternative for the wedding if you don't let me do this."

Lacey glanced at Mick and he gave her a small nod in return. "If you're sure. Then yes, and thank you, Bess."

CHAPTER 14

Her eyes still shut, Maeve savored the feel of Jack's arms around her and the cozy feeling of being nestled into his hard body.

It felt so right. *Too* right. And utterly addictive.

The day had been a blur of activity—rushing to the store to get groceries, packing up a picnic lunch with the epicurean guidance of Bess, and stuck in a logjam of traffic on her way to Jack's house. Annapolis was packed with Navy families and tourists who had come to watch the spectacle of the Blue Angels fighter pilots flying over Annapolis to honor the Academy graduates.

One of Jack's Academy friends who had left the Navy for civilian life had invited them onto his family's boat to see the air show, and with cars moving at a snail's pace downtown, she and Jack had arrived at their dock only minutes before they were due to set sail.

Jack had been right. She couldn't imagine a better way to witness the jaw-dropping show. The jets cut low through the sky, seeming only a few feet above their sailboat's mast from its anchorage in the harbor. The sheer power of the jets made the water itself vibrate underneath them. It was dizzying and humbling at the same time.

Her eyes opened slowly to the sight of a red maple tree casting a late day shadow on them both as they snuggled in Jack's hammock. A brisk breeze sent ripples along the Severn River just a few feet away, a beacon to some Annapolitans to catch a late-day sail. But for Maeve, she was content on land for the rest of the evening, with Jack's warmth protecting her from the cool breeze.

"Did you have fun today?" he murmured, seeming only seconds away from blissful sleep.

"Mmhmm."

"Pretty incredible, isn't it?"

"Yeah. I can't believe they can fly so close together without crashing. My heart was in my throat half the time."

"No. I meant Todd's boat. Incredible. 62-footer. Two forward cabins. All the systems you'd ever want. A beauty like that you could take out on blue water without worrying. She's a beauty." He nestled his face closer to hers, stealing a warm kiss. "The show was pretty good too, though."

"Blue water?"

"The ocean. Not the bay."

She rested her head on his chest. "I never knew you were so into boats."

Jack's laugh felt like a low rumble against her cheek. "Maeve, I'm a Sailor."

"Yeah, I know. But you never talk about sailing."

"Who has time now? When I retire from the Navy, I'm going to buy one just like her."

"Oh, is that the big thing you're saving for? You had mentioned something about that before."

"Did I? Yeah. That's what I want. I always wanted to take some kids from the inner city out on a sailboat. Teach them how to control the power of the wind. There's nothing better. My dad used to take me out when I was a teen. We didn't own one, but our family would rent one on base whenever we came down to Annapolis. I was hooked."

Maeve couldn't have been more surprised. "You mean, like start a nonprofit or something?"

"Yeah."

"You never told me any of this before."

He shrugged. "It's such a long time from now. Just a dream."

"It's a beautiful dream."

"I just keep thinking that if a kid can just feel how amazing it is to sail, it might give them some direction, some hope. And it really helps develop skills like teamwork. I think the only reason I'm so close to my sisters is because we learned how to work together as a crew anytime we were on vacation."

Maeve moved on top of him, encasing his face in her hands. "Jack, you are an amazing man." She kissed him, her tongue touching his, tasting the Sam Adams that now lay empty beneath the hammock. Her lips opened more, tracing her tongue along his teeth, and then playfully nipping his bottom lip. She could feel his body react beneath her.

"Wow, if I knew you'd react this way, I would have told you two years ago," he said as she rested her face back down on his chest.

The blue canvas encased them like a warm cocoon, making it difficult to move. Not that she'd want to.

This was the way to spend an evening and she was determined to enjoy every minute of it. Determined to block from her mind the fact that Jack would be leaving soon, only weeks after they had finally reignited the passion that was between them so long ago.

What a painful waste of time.

His breathing slowed, and she watched his eyes flutter, in a dream. His lashes were long and thick. It was a sin that such eyelashes were wasted on a man. When his eyes were open, she never noticed them. They were merely the frames for his hypnotically green eyes.

The blessed shade of the trees made the waterfront so lovely, even in the sun. Her own backyard was lacking trees. Her grandmother had been an avid vegetable gardener and loved plenty of direct sun.

Barely lifting her head, Maeve glanced up at the oak and the maple that their hammock swung from. They were probably fifty or a hundred years old. Maybe more—Maeve never did have much knowledge about trees. She wondered who had planted them and whether they had any idea their trees would still be standing long after they themselves had passed from this earth.

Trees were lasting. Like love, she couldn't resist thinking. The love her grandparents had for each other. The love Lacey had for Mick. The love she had for Jack that would somehow give her the strength to let him go.

Wait a minute.

"Jack," she whispered.

"Mmmm?" his eyes were still shut and his arm squeezed her tighter.

"Jack."

"What?" his voice murmured.

"I've got an idea."

"Yeah?"

"Tell me if this sounds corny. But I was just thinking about trees."

"Okay. Trees…" He yawned. "Good thing to think about. Now sleep. Or you can start kissing me again. Yeah, that would be nice, too."

Maeve struggled to prop herself up on his chest. "Trees are such nice symbols, you know?"

"Guess so."

"Do you think it would be nice to have Lacey and Mick plant a tree in my backyard as part of the ceremony? Something that will symbolize how their love will grow and last through the years?"

Jack finally opened his eyes. "Lacey would probably love that. Especially since they'll be moving so much. If she planted it in San Diego, chances are, she'd be leaving it behind in a couple years."

"But I'll never sell Gram's house. Well, so long as the clients keep coming, I won't have to, anyway."

"You won't have to." He squeezed her tight, reassuring her. "Mick will say it's sentimental bullshit, you know."

"You think?"

"He's a guy. He's required to say that. Truth is, he'll probably love it. And if it makes Lacey happy, it makes Mick happy. Pretty simple equation." He pulled her face closer and gave her a soft kiss. "So what makes you happy, Maeve?"

"You." She didn't miss a beat answering, and it couldn't have been more truthful. These weeks with him had been the happiest she had ever known.

"You've got me."

For now. "Do you really have to go?" The words escaped her lips before she could stop them. From the look in his eyes, she immediately knew the answer.

"To Little Creek, you mean?"

"Mmhm."

"I got orders. It's a done deal."

"So you can't—like—ask to keep your job here."

"It doesn't work like that in the military," Jack answered, and added, "unfortunately."

"Or maybe ask for a little more time here. Maybe ask for some leave time in between jobs."

"No. I already got my report date. The movers will be coming right after the wedding."

That made her bolt upright. "You haven't even started packing."

"The movers do that for you. They do everything. Wrap everything, pack it in their boxes, load it on a truck. I just sit there and sign the paperwork at the end. I'll keep some stuff with me so I'll have it when I arrive. A couple uniforms. Shave kit. My kayak so I can hit the water when I get down there. The truck usually shows up a lot later than I do because they put a few other moves on the same truck."

Maeve rested her head back on his chest. She didn't want him to see the tears welling up in her eyes. But when a tear fell onto his shirt, he must have noticed.

"Maeve, just because I'm going doesn't mean this has to end, you know."

She swallowed. "Of course. I know." But she didn't. She knew that his departure from Annapolis would be the beginning of the end. With all the miles between them, he'd go on with his life, meet someone new. Someone more appropriate for his future.

And so would she. Eventually.

"I'm only a few hours' drive away. It will be hard to get up here at times because I'll be on twenty-four alert. But when I have a weekend off, I'll be here. If I'm invited, that is."

She forced a smile. "You're always invited. You know that."

"And I'll have plenty of room for you to stay with me so you can come visit."

"Sure. Sure I will." She tried to sound sincere. She loved the idea of visiting him. But would that just prolong the inevitable?

"I'll be at sea a lot. But—" He shifted fully toward her, his eyes meeting hers. "—I'd love to know you would be there waiting when I got back."

She stared, lost in his eyes, and drowning in his words. How could she answer that? The truth was, she'd always be there, waiting for him. Even when someone else replaced her and he settled with the family he always dreamed about… she'd still be waiting for him, waiting to hear that he was all right, safe, happy.

Her love wouldn't end. The realization shouldn't have come as a surprise. She had grown so used to his laugh, his company out on her back porch, the way he could make her smile even when things seemed at their worst. She loved the comfort of knowing he was there, as though somehow his very presence made her stronger.

She had known all along she loved him. But she hadn't realized till now that the love she had for him was the same kind her grandparents had had for each other. The same kind her parents had. The kind that lasts.

How would she go on after she let him go? And if she loved him, she had to. She had seen what it was like with Bess—that moment of Abigail's birth. That moment when suddenly the earth shifted and all that was important was the life of this precious child.

Even being Bess's friend and Abigail's godmother, Maeve had felt it. She couldn't imagine how much stronger the feeling could be if the child had been her own.

She wanted that for Jack.

"Will you?" His words snapped her back, and she stared into his questioning eyes.

"I'll always be there for you, Jack. Nothing will ever change that."

"Good." He rested his head back down onto the stiff canvas pillow, a contented grin on his face. A laugh escaped him.

"What's so funny?"

"I'm suddenly picturing Lacey trying to plant a tree in a big white dress."

Maeve sighed, feeling grateful to be distracted from her own thoughts. "Hadn't thought of that. Maybe it's not such a good idea."

"Let's look on the internet and see what other people have done. I can't imagine you're the first to come up with the idea of a tree planting ceremony."

"Are you saying I can't come up with an original idea?"

"Maeve, in the age of the internet, no idea is original."

She laughed, noticing how once again, he had made her smile at a time she thought things were hopeless.

CHAPTER 15

"That's the dumbest idea I've ever heard of." With a stack of files in his hands, Mick stared at Jack, baffled, as they packed their belongings in the small office they had shared for two school years.

"Well, don't tell that to Maeve. She really likes it. And I'm betting Lacey will like it, too." Jack wrapped packing paper around the framed photo of his family. "It's symbolism, Mick. Tons of people do it. Just punch in 'tree planting ceremony' online. A tree is something lasting, something that grows, you know the deal."

Mick had been surly since he and Lacey had arrived back from San Diego yesterday, still chest-deep in negotiations over a house they had bid on, and grumbling about sellers with unreasonable expectations. "Yeah, I understand the tree part," he replied. "But wouldn't it make more sense to plant it?"

Shaking his head, Jack put the wrapped picture in a cardboard box, gently pressing it down to make more room. He had no idea he had accumulated so much stuff in his office. "Not with Lacey in a wedding gown. Of course not." He grabbed a coffee mug his niece had made him, and dumped the pens that filled it onto his desk. "You take a sapling, put it in a pot. You water it. She waters it. Sometimes couples have their parents water it. And you're pronounced husband and wife."

"A sapling? I thought you said we'd plant a tree."

"A sapling is a baby tree. You know, a few inches high."

"Well, I think it should be a tree. Something that won't get mowed over by a lawnmower by accident. You know, about six or so feet." Mick dropped some papers into a box in front of him. "And how is it meaningful if we don't actually plant it the same day?"

"God, you're difficult. I can't believe Lacey agreed to marry you," Jack muttered.

"I'm serious, Jack. I like my idea better. We get one of those crepe myrtles—you know, the ones that bloom in late summer. Lacey always says they remind her of me because they were in bloom when I got back from Afghanistan and proposed."

Jack leaned back in his chair, stunned. "So you *are* a sentimental, after all."

"Not sentimental. I just remember that sort of stuff. Gets me out of the doghouse when I do something stupid. You'd be smart to take a lesson from me on that one."

"So you want a crepe myrtle?"

"Yeah. And a nice big one. I'm a SEAL, for God sake. I like things big. Freakin' sapling?

That's just insulting," he finished under his breath.

Jack pressed his lips together in thought as he wrapped another frame. He had to find a way to make this work. Surely a man who had four sisters could manage to fuse male practicality with female sentimentality. "Okay. So we can dig the hole beforehand so it's ready. Then you can put it in there. Won't be too hard even in a dress uniform. Lacey will toss a little soil on it with a shovel."

"And we'll do it at the end of the night so it won't mess up any pictures if Lacey gets a little soil on her. Everything goes to the cleaner afterward anyway."

"All right. We'll run it by Lacey. It would be a nice end to the night. Beats the hell out of a garter toss."

"Yeah. No garter toss," Mick said firmly. "With a bunch of SEALs, it could get violent. They're kind of competitive." Mick pulled out another file and weeded through the papers.

Jack sealed up the cardboard box with shipping tape. The tape still in hand, he stared blankly at the wall for a moment. "Have you ever thought about getting out?"

"Out of the SEALs? Or out of the Navy?"

"Either."

"Nearly every day since Lacey came along."

"Really?"

"That surprises you?"

"Hell, yeah. You're a SEAL. You know, "Ready to Lead. Ready to Follow. Never Quit,'"

Jack prattled off the SEAL motto, putting emphasis on the last two words.

Mick eased back in his chair. "I know. And that motto must have been written by a single guy," he laughed. "Seriously, I'm 33. That's getting old for Special Ops. There's always an end to the road. I can't imagine mine is too far away."

"You could command. Be the next Captain Shey."

"And have no one to go home to at night like him? Hell no. Truth is, if Lacey said she wanted me out tomorrow, I'd be putting in my paperwork within the hour."

"You're serious?"

"Yeah. And I've told her that. She says she knows what she's in for. But no one ever does. She can't imagine what it's like—sending me off to war. Sitting by herself for the next six months or year. Wondering every day whether a Casualty Assistance Calls Officer will show up on her doorstep." He shook his head. "No one knows what that's like till you go through it. And if we have kids? Christ, I don't know how women do it."

"But plenty do."

"Sure, and they have my admiration. They do. But in my team alone, I've seen plenty of damn strong women leave their husbands because it's too much to take. I can't blame them at all. I've heard people say afterward, 'Oh, she knew what she was marrying into.' But that's utter bullshit." His shoulders slumped, as if remembering something bad. He gave himself a little shake. "If Lacey decides she can't take it, then I'm out."

"That shocks the hell out of me."

"Shocks the hell out of me, too. But I love her. And there comes a time when someone else has to play the cowboy." He set a stack of files in a cardboard box. "Why? Are you thinking of getting out?"

"No. Just wishing there was some kind of balance." He moved the box to the lateral filing cabinet and started filling another empty one. "I'm worried about the cancer, Mick. Shit. What if it comes back and I'm away? I can't let her go through that alone."

"Well, if something like that happens, you can talk to your CO and hope for emergency leave. But you probably won't get it if she's just your girlfriend. You'd have better luck if you were married to her."

"You think I should marry her?"

"I didn't say that. I'm just saying that wives have a lot more clout than girlfriends as far as the Navy is concerned. You know the deal."

Jack sat back down in his chair. "It's too early to think about marriage."

Mick scoffed. "I know you, Jack. You've been thinking about it since that day Lacey called me up screaming in my ear that you two finally had sex." He shook his head. "My ear is still ringing from that."

"And that was barely a week ago."

"A week. That's already about a month in military time."

"Military time?"

"Yeah. Military time. Kind of like dog years. I figure us military guys have less time stateside just because we're deployed so much, so it speeds up the clock. We have to make decisions faster. Make use of our time dating more efficiently. Get married. Plan for kids during a time when we can actually be around for the conception."

"You're such a romantic."

Mick grinned. "You know me." He shut the empty drawer in front of him. "A week dating a military guy is like, say, four weeks dating a civilian."

Jack stared blankly, doing calculations in his head. So he had waited thirty-two years to get Maeve back into his bed? No wonder he felt so frustrated. Jack shook his head.

"What? It makes perfect sense," Mick said, taking offense at Jack's reaction.

"No. I mean, yeah. It sort of does, Mick."

"And hell, you've been seeing her at least two or three times a week since I got back from Afghanistan last summer. Right?"

Jack shrugged. "It's different as friends."

"I'm not saying to rush anything. But it's not like we all don't know where this is headed." Mick angled his head. "Or am I wrong?"

Jack didn't mistake the mildly threatening tone. Mick played the role of big brother to Maeve well enough. "What?"

"I mean, Lacey told me that Maeve can't have kids. And everyone within ten-mile radius knows that kids were next on your check-off list."

"Christ, Mick, what do you take me for? I could marry any woman and find out that we can't have kids. I might be shooting blanks myself for all I know. I'd like to marry a woman. Not a uterus."

"Ugh. Can you cut the female organs out of the conversation, please? We all didn't grow up with four sisters."

Jack narrowed his eyes, spotting Mick's vulnerability. "You're such a pussy. You break out in a sweat if Lacey even tells you she has cramps."

Mick held up a warning finger. "Quit it, Jack."

"What's the matter, Mick? Not comfortable talking about ovaries?"

Mick lunged for him, capturing him in a headlock. Jack sputtered for air, laughing as he struggled, forcing his chin down till he flipped Mick onto the floor in front of him.

"Damn, Jack." Flat on the hard floor, Mick was all smiles. "That was actually good. You finally started learning something from me."

Still laughing, Jack put his head between his legs, catching his breath. "Took me two years. You're an asshole, Mick. But I'm going to miss the hell out of you."

"Me, too." He raised an eyebrow at Jack, watching him lift a box and head for the door. "But I'm dead serious. If you break Maeve's heart, then she'll go straight to Lacey for support, and that means I'd be the one stuck hosting an 'I hate men fest' on my living room couch. I'll kick your ass for that."

Jack stopped in the doorway. "If anyone's heart gets broken in this picture, I have a feeling it will be mine."

CHAPTER 16

Maeve held Jack's arm as he escorted her to their seats in the Navy-Marine Corps Memorial Stadium—his left arm, as he directed, so that his right would be free to salute.

"That security was crazy," she commented, knowing her eyes must have been saucer-sized from the chaos and excitement that engulfed her since they had arrived to watch the mids graduate. Her own commencement ceremony from design school, in a small performing arts center tucked away in Greenwich Village, had been nothing like this.

"It's always tight, but having the President here to speak this year makes it a little harder."

The President. She couldn't help but be a bit dazzled by the idea of seeing him first-hand. It didn't matter which way she leaned at the last election, usually flip-flopping between parties because neither seemed to get much done. But something about being this close to the leader of a world power was just humbling to her.

Yet she couldn't help noticing that the people around her seemed more excited to see their loved ones receive their diplomas than to hear the President speak.

"It's not just about the diploma," Jack explained, when she pointed out her observation to him. "They're being commissioned as officers in the Navy and Marine Corps. It's a huge moment for them, taking the oath to defend their country. And it takes four years of grueling work to get to this point for them."

"Do you remember yours well?"

"I remember every minute. Taking the oath. I graduated with distinction so I was one of the first to get my diploma. But it still seemed like an eternity till they got to my name." He smiled, remembering. "I'm not overly emotional, you know. My sisters would razz me too much if I were. But I got seriously choked up. It changes your life." He looked at her meaningfully. "And then I met you that night. I remember every minute of that, too." He touched her knee, and she longed to kiss him, but knew that PDAs would be frowned on in this environment.

A bugle sounded in the distance.

They stood, and Jack saluted as the President entered the stadium to the sound of "Hail to the Chief." She jumped with a start at the sound of cannons firing. Jack held his salute until the last shot was fired.

They remained standing as they sang the National Anthem, then lowering their heads in prayer as the benediction was given. Maeve could feel herself getting choked up, just as Jack had been so many years ago, hearing the words of the chaplain, words that reminded her of the risk that awaited every one of the mids who stood in formation in the center of the stadium.

No, this wasn't any ordinary commencement. And none of these graduates were ordinary. What did it take, she wondered? What was the calling that made someone raise their hand and voluntarily serve their country during a time of such uncertainty?

Maeve glanced around her to the families surrounding her. There was pride in their eyes. She looked for the worry that she imagined she would feel, if it had been her child taking this path. But she couldn't see it. It would come later, she imagined.

The Superintendent spoke first, with words even more inspiring, in Maeve's opinion, than the President's speech that came later. Then the moment that brought tears to many of the family members she saw, when the mids took the oath. First, the Assistant Commandant of the Marine Corps administered the oath to those who had chosen to become Marines. Then, the Chief of Naval Operations administered the oath to those becoming ensigns in the Navy.

She glanced at Jack and his eyes were a world away, as if he was remembering his own moment standing at the center of the stadium. The words he had said then had shaped his life. Still wearing the uniform, he would say the words again today if he were called to do so. He was Navy, through and through.

The oath was completed by a rousing "I do" from the Navy's newest officers. They were mids no longer.

Maeve bit her lip, blinking back tears. She didn't know a single one of the new Navy ensigns and Marine second lieutenants there. But she felt immeasurable pride in being part of this moment.

Yes, this was hell-and-gone from a normal commencement. It should be a day of national pride. And… *Crap*. She hadn't even thought to put out her flag.

"You okay?" Jack whispered.

"I'm fine. Just feeling like I take so much for granted."

He looked like he was about to ask her something, when all attention went to the Academic Dean and Provost as he called the first name to receive his diploma—with distinction, Maeve noted just as Jack had been. In his uniform, the young man shaking the President's hand looked so much like Jack that first time they had met.

Families and friends stood as their sons' and daughters' names were called, a Navy tradition to recognize their role in supporting the new officers.

After the last name was called, they rose again, this time to sing "Our Navy, Blue and Gold." Maeve looked to her program for the words, and sang it, completely off-key since she had never heard it before. But in this enthusiastic crowd, no one would ever notice or care.

The crowd gave three cheers, and then she saw it—the moment that she had seen captured in photographs so many times. The new officers tossed their hats up into the air.

She couldn't stop smiling.

Even an hour later, stuck in a mess of traffic on the way home from the stadium, she still had a silly grin on her face.

Jack glanced over at her at a stoplight. "So I take it you enjoyed it?"

"Oh, Jack—yes," she answered. "Do you know how remarkable it all is? All the tradition and patriotism? Most people never get to be a part of something so great, so huge."

Jack nodded sagely. "There's a heritage that comes with being in the armed forces. You are taught to think of yourselves as being part of a long line of history that started in 1775, before the Revolutionary War even began. There's pride there, but also all the pressure that comes with it."

"I can imagine."

"How about we go to Eagle's Point again for dinner tonight? You're all dressed up. I want to show you off."

"Too expensive. How about O'Toole's?"

"I don't care what it costs. Besides, anyplace closer to downtown will be packed tonight."

"If you're sure. But do you think we need reservations?"

"I'm in uniform. Do you think they'd say no to me?"

Maeve glanced over at him, looking delicious in his Navy whites. "I guess not," she agreed.

Lord knows she had no intention of saying 'no' to him tonight either.

CHAPTER 17

Half awake, half asleep, Jack could barely register the sound of Maeve's steady breathing on top of him, or the gentle weight of her head on his chest.

There was no reason to open his eyes yet. With the school year over, he could finally start a weekday slowly, skipping PT and his usual morning rush for coffee. He could hold Maeve in his arms as long as he wanted, without the annoying scream of an alarm clock waking him.

A dream called to him, and he let it take over his thoughts. In it, he was with Maeve. They were on the beach in Fort Story, Virginia, the golden sand warm beneath a couple towels he had carelessly tossed on the ground.

He'd have to take her there one day, he decided in his half-conscious state. She'd love it—watching the dolphins racing along the coastline, feeling the ocean breeze on her skin and in her hair, as she relaxed on a chaise along the dunes.

If he could just convince her to come visit him, he could have the time he needed with her to show her how life could be together. He could see the skepticism in her eyes when he talked about the future, even in the short-term. With a divorce behind her, he didn't imagine she'd be eager to skip down the aisle again.

In his near sleep state, his brain was calculating. Four days left. Ninety-six hours. About sixty-four of that she'd be awake. And with all the wedding guests flying in today, bachelor party at O'Toole's, rehearsal dinner, wedding... he'd probably only get Maeve to himself for twelve or so hours of that.

Not much time left.

But he wouldn't worry about that. Not now. Right now he would lie in bed and let the images of the sea lull him back to a dream of Maeve relaxing in his arms on the beach.

Just about to fall into a deep slumber, a knock at the door made him sit up straight in bed.

Maeve's eyes cracked open. "Was that the door?"

The knock sounded again.

He kissed her on the forehead. "Yeah. Go back to sleep, I'll get it."

Glancing at the clock on his nightstand, he slipped on some shorts, and ran his hand through his hair. His reflection in the mirror proved that even with a short military cut, a guy could still get serious bed-head. As his hand brushed against his stubble, he hoped it wasn't some Admiral at the door. His beard was way out of tolerance.

Opening the door, he barely recognized the woman on the other side, her eyes puffy and cheeks stained with tears. "Lacey?"

"Hi, Jack." She sniffled.

"Are you okay?" Lame words, he knew. It was pretty clear she wasn't okay.

"Yes." Her face curled up and tears started to pour from her eyes. "No. Is Maeve here? She turned her phone off."

"Yeah. Come on in."

When Maeve emerged from his bedroom, Lacey darted into her arms and sobbed.

"Oh my God, honey. What's the matter?" Maeve said, sounding as maternal as a woman could get.

"I can't do it, Maeve. I can't get married."

Oh, shit. Jack took two steps backward.

"What are you talking about? Did you guys have a fight?" Maeve's voice was gentle and calming, a side of her that Jack rarely saw.

"No. No, I didn't even talk to him. He's at the gym. I left him a message."

Ouch. Jack headed to the kitchen to put on a pot of coffee. Company was coming.

"Saying what?" Maeve handed her a tissue.

Lacey blew. "That I'm too scared. That I just can't do this."

"It's just cold feet," Maeve assured her.

"It's not. It's statistics," she sobbed.

Jack stood baffled. He had taken plenty of stats in school. Maybe he could actually be of use in this conversation. "Okay. What statistics are you talking about exactly?"

"Divorce. We don't stand a chance, you know? It always ends in divorce."

"It doesn't," Jack offered. "Fifty percent isn't 'always,' Lacey. My parents are still together. Maeve's are. Your parents are still together."

Lacey reached for another tissue. "Vi's getting divorced."

"Oh," Jack said, finally understanding. Vi hadn't even been married a year yet. The ink on their marriage certificate was barely dry. "And that's making you panic about your own wedding."

"Mmhm." She wiped her eyes. "She told me this morning when I picked her up at the airport. She didn't want to tell me. But I asked her why he wasn't coming to the wedding and I kept pushing for the real answer, you know? She kept saying he was working. But geez, what kind of a man would suddenly need to work rather than see your sister-in-law get married, right?" She blew her nose. "I mean, I flew all the way down to Palm Beach to see them get married. You'd think that bastard could make it up here from Atlanta. I knew something was going on." She took the cup of coffee Jack offered and sipped. "So she finally gave in and told me. He cheated on her."

"Son of a bitch." Maeve and Jack said in unison.

"Yeah. He cheated. On Vi." She sipped again, seeming somehow stronger armed with caffeine. Anger flashed in her eyes. "On Vi! I mean, who the hell would cheat on her? She's gorgeous. She's smart. Successful. She's every man's fantasy."

Jack's temper boiled. Assholes like this guy gave good men a bad reputation. "Lacey, when a guy cheats, it has nothing to do with the woman. It has everything to do with the man. He would have cheated no matter who she was, what she looked like, or what she did."

His words fell on deaf ears.

She sat on the sofa. "And you, Maeve. It happened to you. God, when I think about that prick who left you, I want to rip his damn balls off."

Jack fought the urge to cross his legs. He knew her bark was worse than her bite. "Mick would never cheat on you."

"How do you know that? How do *I* know that?"

Maeve sat beside her. "You know it, Lacey. You wouldn't be with him now if you had the slightest doubt."

"But he'll be gone so much, you know? If Vi's husband couldn't be trusted—and they were around each other all the time. They even worked together."

"And you're worried because Mick will be deployed so much." Jack sat on the coffee table, opposite Lacey.

"How could I not be?"

Jack lifted her chin up so that he could meet her eyes. "There's going to be plenty for you to worry about in the next few years, Lacey. But Mick cheating isn't one of them. He'd die first. I'm not being dramatic. I'm being factual. Hell, I wouldn't stand up in his wedding if I had any doubts. Marriage is serious shit in my family."

"Marriage is shit. Period," Lacey grumbled, dropping her gaze.

Maeve drew in a breath, holding her hand to her mouth. "Oh, God, I've done this to you, haven't I?"

"No."

She shook her head. "I did. For years now, I've been blasting marriage like it's public enemy #1."

"You said it because it's the truth."

"It's not the truth. And don't let your bitter, spiteful—" Maeve smiled briefly, "—albeit shockingly beautiful friend ruin your ideas about marriage. Half the reason I've been so bitter about my own divorce is because I had such high expectations. My parents have a wonderful marriage. And my grandparents—God, theirs was one destined for a Hallmark channel movie. I wanted that. And because I wanted it so badly, I think I rushed into it with the first guy who asked."

Maeve glanced at Jack briefly, and he wondered for a moment if it was longing he saw in her eyes. Or maybe it was his own wishful thinking. He stood to get a cup of coffee for himself. If he was going to deal with anymore of this, he'd do it better with caffeine in his veins.

Behind him, Maeve's voice was so sincere Jack could barely recognize it. "At its best, marriage is a beautiful thing. Imagine, finding someone you want to commit to forever. Vowing before your friends and family to do just that. Knowing that you will have each other during the good times and the bad times. Growing old together." He heard her pause, and her voice softened, as though her words were only meant to be heard by Lacey. "If I could, I'd do it again in a heartbeat."

Pouring coffee from the carafe, Jack missed, a trickle of coffee splattering alongside his mug. He was glad to be facing the other way so that Maeve and Lacey couldn't see his jaw hitting the counter.

Maeve felt that way about marriage? Till now, he had thought it might take months or even years to convince her to give it a try again.

His mind wandered to his conversation with Mick a few days ago. "We all know where this is headed," Mick had said. Damned if he wasn't right.

Jack snapped out of it at the sound of someone pounding on his door, right on cue. *Speaking of Mick.*

Maeve tilted her head in Lacey's direction. "Well, my, my. I can't imagine who that could be at this hour."

More tears fell from Lacey's eyes. "I'm such a wreck. Why would he even want to marry someone like me?"

"Because he loves you more than life itself. Don't throw that away just because *some* men are asses, and *some* marriages don't work. Yours will. I wouldn't let you get married to him if I didn't believe that."

Lacey fell apart at the seams, hugging Maeve. "I love you, Maeve."

"I love you, too."

Sighing, Jack picked up the fresh cup he had just poured and carried it to the door. With four sisters, he was pretty accustomed to this level of sap. Mick was going to need the coffee more than him. "Want me to talk to him first?"

Lacey shook her head, and Jack opened the door.

Mick stood in the doorway, looking like hell, his t-shirt and shorts drenched in the sweat of his usual morning workout. "Lacey?" he asked as his expectant eyes met her teary ones.

"It's just cold feet, Mick," Maeve quickly assured him. "Vi's getting divorced and Lacey panicked."

"Oh, baby—" he started.

Mick took two steps toward Lacey and Jack blocked him.

"You are not sitting on my sofa smelling like that. I get enough shit from Maeve about that sofa as it is. I don't need it smelling like the combatives mats at the gym."

Lacey stood and let herself be wrapped in Mick's sweaty arms.

Jack eased up to Maeve's side. "She must really love him—to hug him smelling like that."

Maeve grinned. "Yeah, if we ever get in a fight while you're at the gym, promise to shower before you come home to work things out, okay?"

"Deal."

CHAPTER 18

Squinting at her reflection in the mirror, Maeve flipped it over to the magnifying side, and applied her eye makeup with the prowess of a master. She sighed briefly at the sight of two tiny new wrinkles alongside her eyes that had emerged overnight.

Frowning, she thought it unfair that just when wrinkles were starting to appear, she had started needing a magnifying mirror to apply her makeup, making the tiny lines seem even bigger.

But there was no justice in aging. She glanced briefly at the tiny bottles of miracle creams scattered around her sink, which provided no miracles at all.

In the battle between skin and gravity, gravity always won.

Bess popped her head into the bathroom. "You're still putting on makeup?"

Maeve cocked her head. "Well, since I had to do yours and Lacey's first, yes, I am."

Grinning ear to ear, Bess looked at herself in the mirror. "You did an awesome job. I barely look like myself."

Maeve couldn't agree with her more. In her vibrant bridesmaid dress, with her fiery red curls framing her porcelain face, Bess didn't look like a harried mom. She looked 23. And beautiful.

Maeve wished she could get Bess to dress up like this more. Privately, Maeve vowed to burn every set of worn-down sweats that Bess owned and force her to do some shopping after the wedding. Even the clearance racks at Target offered more stylish options than Bess's bleak wardrobe.

Turning back to the mirror, she focused her attention on her lips, drawing a delicate line of red with her lip pencil and filling it in with a dewy cherry gloss. She smacked her lips and, not pulling her eyes from her own image, couldn't resist asking, "Do you think I'm vain, Bess?"

Bess tossed her head back in laughter.

Maeve stared at her, brows arched.

"Oh," Bess paled. "You're serious. I thought you were joking."

Maeve frowned. "So, I take it that's a 'yes.'"

Bess bit her lip, and Maeve winced, seeing her friend's perfect lipstick now smeared on her front tooth. "Well, maybe just a little vain. And in a nice way."

Maeve stepped back a foot, flipped the mirror over, and smiled as the tiny lines around her eyes disappeared. To hell with magnification. "In a nice way," she repeated thoughtfully. "I guess that's okay, then."

Bess brightened. "Absolutely. A little vanity is a good thing. Hey—it got me out of sweats and into a nice dress today, right?"

"And you look gorgeous. Seriously. I don't think I've ever seen you looking better, except when you had just given birth to Abby. But that was a different kind of gorgeous."

"I should hope so. And speaking of gorgeous, Lacey's dress is on, but Vi can't get it laced up right. Can you help? I've got to get Abby in her dress."

"I'm on my way." Maeve glanced at her reflection and gave a little nod. Good enough. Best not to outdo the bride, anyway, she thought, stepping into the hall on her way to Lacey's room.

The house was already abuzz. Half her downstairs furniture had been whisked away to temporary storage to allow for more seating for the cocktail hour. And now with staff doing the set up, the noise echoed its way up the stairs, rattling her nerves.

Edith was downstairs helping direct traffic. The older woman had proven to be a Godsend from the moment she walked through the door that morning. With all her experience as a doctor's wife planning hospital fundraisers, Edith was just the person to make sure things went smoothly.

Mick had hit the lottery when he had gotten Edith as a sponsor back in his Academy days. After he and Lacey moved, Maeve made a promise to herself to keep in touch with Edith. Maeve owed her so much after today, and she had to admit, she found Edith's presence a steady comfort and her advice was always spot-on.

So much like Gram, Maeve couldn't help thinking as her eyes caught a glimpse of her grandmother's picture in the hallway.

Food was in abundance in the kitchen, waiting on warming plates and in chafing dishes till the time it would be served. The smells wafted up the stairs, making Maeve's stomach growl even though she had just eaten lunch.

Turning the corner into Lacey's room, the flashes of the photographer's camera took her aback till she spotted Lacey, looking radiant and stressed at the same time. Her dress sparkled, with organza spilling down to the floor in long, dreamy swirls.

Vi stood alongside her, bent at the hip, struggling to lace up the gown's corset. Her make-up was perfect, and Maeve expected nothing less from someone who spent so much time in front of a TV camera. But her hair today wasn't its usual all-business updo. It covered her shoulders in long, loose curls.

"I heard you might need some help," Maeve offered.

"This corset is ridiculous," Vi muttered. "Why don't they just use a zipper?"

Maeve laughed, nudging her to the side, ready to take over. "Because it's a bridal gown. Not a ski jacket."

With the bow finally tied, Maeve turned Lacey toward her. "God, honey. You look like an angel."

"Mick's going to fall over when he sees you walk down that aisle." Vi grinned as she held both her sister's hands, and the camera flashed in response. "Of course, he looked pretty amazing himself. Those Navy uniforms are damn sexy. All those medals." She fanned her ring-free hand in front of her face.

Maeve tilted her head, someone's image popping into her brain. "If you like medals, then there's someone I definitely want to see you dancing with tonight." She glanced at Lacey, who seemed to have read her mind.

"Captain Shey?" Lacey whispered quietly when Vi's back was turned. "He'd be the rebound guy," she warned.

Maeve let her Southern drawl slip out. "And my, my. What a lovely rebound he'd be."

Lacey laughed as Abigail toddled into the room, a cherub in white, crowned with flowers. "Oh, little princess. You look so pretty."

Delighted, Abigail tottered back to Bess and thumped on her mother's thigh with her chubby hand. "Pretty," she said, looking at her mother.

Bess's mouth dropped open. "Her first word," she said breathlessly.

Tearing up, Maeve put her hand to her chest. "Oh, God. Here goes all of our eye makeup."

Lacey walked over to Bess and hugged her, the photographer snapping photos from behind. "She's right, honey. You are so pretty. Don't you ever forget that, okay?"

Bess was bawling now. "I won't."

Maeve sniffled, reaching for a tissue. The first tissue of many she'd need today, she imagined. She let out a slow breath, trying to compose herself.

"And now," Vi said, the only one who wasn't streaked with tears, "for something old." She reached into her pocket and handed Lacey a simple ring of white gold with three tiny diamonds sparkling on it. "It's from Mom, Lacey. She wanted you to have this. It was her engagement ring from Dad, back before they had any money and could replace it with the rock she has now." Vi tossed back a laugh, slipping it onto Lacey's right hand. "I know she doesn't say it much, but she's really proud of you."

At that, Vi's composure broke, her voice cracking. "And so am I." She hugged her briefly and then darted a look at Maeve. "Oh, God. Where are those tissues?"

Maeve handed her the box. "For something new, we'll have to settle for the dress. But for something borrowed, I think I have just the thing." She reached into her jewelry box and pulled out her grandmother's ruby and diamond necklace and earrings that flashed rose red to match Lacey's bouquet.

Lacey glowed as Maeve draped the necklace against her, the jewelry sparkling against her creamy skin.

Setting Abigail down on the bed, Bess came over to Lacey, her outstretched hand holding a small box. "And for something blue, this is from Maeve, Abigail, and me. To remember your time with us in Annapolis."

Her eyes already filled, Lacey took the box in hand. Flipping it open, her breath caught. "Oh my God, you guys. It's beautiful."

Maeve took the delicate bracelet of sapphires in white gold, and fastened it over Lacey's wrist.

Brimming with emotion, her friend's hands were shaking. Maeve stilled them in her own. "Now, you are perfection," Maeve said. "And if I'm not mistaken, I think perfection could use a glass of champagne."

With the sun sinking lower in the crystal clear sky, Maeve stood among her dearest friends gazing at her backyard, speckled with candlelight and flower petals, as Lacey walked up the aisle.

Don't cry. Don't cry. She didn't dare look at Bess, whom she guessed would be drenched with tears by now. She pressed her lips together, struggling to keep it together. Her eyes darted to Jack across the aisle, looking completely composed in his uniform, as her first tear fell.

He smiled tenderly in response.

On her father's arm, Lacey looked calmer than Maeve had ever seen her. Her eyes were locked on Mick, looking breathtaking in his Navy choker whites, with his medals glimmering in the evening sun. They were so right together.

Yet it still somehow broke Maeve's heart. Her mind flashed to the day she had met Lacey—at her grandmother's funeral of all places. Damned if she didn't feel Gram's presence here right now, holding back the clouds and ensuring a perfect evening for Maeve's dear friend.

Maeve glanced at the house adorned with festive white buntings that blew in the breeze. She would have sold this house if it hadn't been for Lacey. She'd still be living in Baltimore, probably working at the same dead-end firm, aching from the pain of divorce and memory of cancer.

And Jack? Jack would still be a memory from her 29th year—a weekend fling that would make every man since then pale in comparison.

When Lacey reached the end of the aisle, Maeve took her bouquet so that bride and groom could join hands. She noticed Lacey's hands weren't shaking any more. She was strong and certain and secure. She was right where she was supposed to be. At Mick's side.

Even if that took her far from Annapolis, Maeve knew it was right. She'd let her friend go.

Her eyes met Jack's again. There was so much letting go to be done in her future, she thought, her mind drifting to a place called Little Creek where he'd plant his roots for the next years. She watched him, his face solemn as he watched Lacey and Mick say their vows.

For a man like Jack, they weren't words. They were an oath.

A little hand tugged on Maeve's dress. Glancing down, Maeve kissed her hand and then planted it on Abby's forehead, and the child beamed up at her in return. Her heart warmed. She'd let go of Lacey because Lacey loved Mick. She'd let go of Jack because she loved him.

But never you, my sweet goddaughter. I'll never let go of you.

"You may kiss the bride," the chaplain said. They kissed, Lacey's hands holding Mick's face as his arms wrapped around her waist. The cameras flashed and tears fell. Maeve dared to look at Bess, who was all but falling apart next to her. Maeve gave her arm a gentle squeeze and handed her the tissue she had hidden underneath her bouquet.

"I'm really happy," Bess whispered. "I don't know why I'm crying."

"Because it's a wedding." Maeve smiled as she took Jack's arm to walk down the aisle.

At the end of the aisle, Jack moved her off to the side and kissed her.

"What was that for?"

"You looked like you needed it. Are you okay?"

Maeve sighed as she looked at the crowd starting to filter out of their chairs. "I'll be okay when we pull this night off without a hitch. I'm going to make sure we're ready for cocktail hour in the house."

"Don't. Edith has it under control. She said she'd chase us out if she saw any of the wedding party in there till the photos were done."

He took her by the hand, following the flashes of light to the photographer, who was already doing the customary poses in front of the camera.

Bride's side of the family. Groom's side of the family. Groomsmen.

Maeve's breath hitched at the sight of Jack surrounded by his fellow Sailors. The two other groomsmen were SEALs, like Mick. Yet in Maeve's opinion, Jack looked more impressive in his uniform than both of them put together.

Her mind wandered to an image of Jack at 22, fresh out of the Academy. His shoulders seemed twice the size as they used to be, and he seemed… taller, as though something about the years had given him a more intimidating stature. He was so different from the young man she had met so long ago.

The Silver Star that had been pinned on him just weeks ago glimmered on his uniform, just one medal in a sea of others. She'd have to ask him what they all meant one day.

One day. It would have to be soon. There weren't many days left.

"And now the bridal party," the photographer said, and Maeve took her place alongside Vi and Bess.

"Is my mascara okay?" Bess whispered, panic in her tear-moistened eyes.

"Perfect. I told you waterproof was the way to go. Now just smile. I'm getting you a shot of bourbon after this."

Bess laughed just as the camera snapped. And snapped. And snapped again. Maeve's face was starting to cramp. She looked at Lacey, who shot her a desperate look.

"Is it possible to get a charley horse in your cheeks?" Lacey asked.

"You're doing fine," Maeve assured her, and held up a finger to the photographer to have her wait. "Stop smiling a second and lick your upper front teeth. Better?"

"Ah, yes. Thanks," Lacey said, slapping on a smile again.

Jack sidled up to her after they were done. "Old beauty pageant trick?"

Maeve laughed. "How'd you guess?"

His hand lightly traced her back. "Do you have any idea how beautiful you are?" He kissed her deeply, his hand at the small of her back holding her close.

The feeling of his lips tantalizing, she nudged his mouth open, touching his tongue lightly and tasting the champagne he must have had before the ceremony. He pulled her closer, till her body was flush with his, and she could feel his arousal low against her belly. She toyed with his tongue, savoring the moment of escape from the chaos of the wedding, and finally pulling away, let out a low purr.

Jack's eyes were at half-mast as he smiled at her. "I've waited all night to do that. I knew you'd kill me if I messed up your makeup before all the photos were done."

"You know me so well."

"Maeve, it's frightening as hell to think how well I know you." He tucked a loose tendril of her hair behind her ear. "I know how much it's hurting you to see Lacey move away. I know how much your heart swelled when you walked Abby down that aisle with her little flower girl bouquet."

Maeve bit her lip, nodding.

"I know how much you worry about Bess. And I think I know how much you love me. Am I right?"

"Yes." Her voice was husky, and more than anything, she wanted to pull him close again rather than going inside for cocktail hour.

"Good." He leaned into her ear, his voice low and tempting. "Because I also know a few of your favorite places to be kissed. And I plan on confirming this tonight."

His lips met hers again, teasing, tasting, and tempting her to sneak him upstairs to her room right now. She couldn't wait to be alone with him.

Pulling back, he touched his finger to her lips. "Now how about we go sample some of that food Bess whipped up?"

That's not what she'd prefer to sample right now. But it would have to do... until later.

The moon hung low in the sky, casting its reflection onto the Bay and lending its soft glow to the crepe myrtle that had been planted by Lacey and Mick that night. Maeve smiled at the memory, only briefly wishing that Lacey would be here to see it blossom later in the summer.

Standing underneath the arbor, thick with abundant white roses still clinging to it, she didn't even have to look at her watch to know it was long past midnight.

The night had been perfect.

Images of the evening danced in her mind like snapshots that she would hold close to her heart forever. The sword arch, with Jack at the helm. The surprise on Lacey's face when he smacked her on her rear with his sword and said, "Welcome to the Navy, Mrs. Ryan," a Navy tradition. Maeve hoped the photographer had managed to capture that moment.

Their first dance to Ella Fitzgerald's sultry voice. Watching Abby jump in glee when the DJ played Electric Slide. Seeing Vi on the dance floor, wrapped up contentedly in Joe Shey's arms.

And that moment when Maeve's eyes met Lacey's, as she waved from the limousine that whisked them off to DC for two nights in the honeymoon suite at a swank hotel, compliments of Edith. That moment when a new chapter in Lacey's life had begun.

And mine, Maeve pondered, thinking how much emptier her house would be without her friend. Lacey and Mick would be leaving for San Diego to close on a house shortly after they returned from their DC getaway. Then they'd be off to a Hawaiian honeymoon, and after, Lacey would return to her new West Coast home, not Maeve's house in Annapolis.

"Gorgeous, are you tired?"

Maeve jumped at the voice of Jack behind her.

"Because you've been running through my dreams all night."

He swept her into his arms in a dip, and she remembered that day in her kitchen. Only six weeks ago, yet it seemed like a lifetime had passed. Only this time, his lips met hers, setting her heart aflame. Still holding her, his mouth moved to her neck, and down to where her bare skin met the red taffeta of her strapless dress.

Suddenly, her fatigue vanished. "Maybe we should go inside," she offered suggestively.

"Not yet," he said. "There's something I need to say to you." He took both her hands, first kissing one, then the other. "Maeve, that day two years ago when I saw you at O'Toole's, I felt like I had one opportunity to make something right."

"What do you mean?"

"I should have tracked you down, Maeve. Eight years ago. I should have pounded on your grandmother's door and demanded your number. But I was young and cocky as hell. I thought you'd call."

Maeve laughed. "But I was young and stupid as hell, and thought I'd do better to find someone who was ready to settle down."

"Yeah. But then by some twist of fate, you fell back into my life. And it took me nearly two years to figure out that I even stood a chance with you. Two years." He shook his head. "And now I'm leaving."

Maeve brushed her hand along his cheek. In the low light, his face looked boyishly handsome. He was so strong, yet in his eyes tonight, Maeve could see vulnerability. She kissed him tenderly, hoping to offer him some of the strength he had always offered her.

Jack touched her chin affectionately. "I wasted too much time. Six years. Then two years. I'm not going to waste time anymore."

He dropped to one knee and Maeve felt the air rush out of her lungs at the sight of a ring in his hand.

"Maeve, I love you with everything I am and everything I ever will be. I know this might seem too soon, and I understand if you want a long engagement, or just some time to think. But I'm not going to leave this town without you knowing exactly how I feel. Not this time. Not again. And what I feel is that I can't stand the thought of my life without you. Marry me. Marry me tomorrow, next week, or next year. I don't care. But just say you'll marry me."

Yes! The word ached to flow past her lips. As her tears fell, she pressed her lips together to keep herself from speaking the one word her heart longed to say.

"Jack. Oh, Jack." She shook her head slowly, a moment of blissful perfection turning into a nightmare more painful than her cancer. More painful than her divorce. Even more painful than the day her Gram died. As the moon disappeared behind a cloud, she sobbed uncontrollably.

"What is it, Maeve?"

"I can't. I can't marry you, Jack."

"Why?"

"Jack, your future is not with me."

"Why not?"

"Because I can't give you children."

"Maeve, we've been over this. I know you can't have kids and that's fine. We can adopt. Or foster. Or we can just spoil the hell out of Abby for the rest of our lives. I don't care."

"But you do," she all be shouted. "For two years now, all I've been hearing is how much you longed for a family. I can't let you give that up for me."

"I'd give anything up for you, Maeve. Don't you get it? I'd give my life for you."

"And I wouldn't want you to. Don't you see? I love you too much." She stepped onto the dock, needing to put some space between them. "I can't go through my life knowing that you sacrificed your dreams of a family for me. I've seen what it's like to bring a baby into this world. I watched it with Abigail. Oh, Jack, it's so beautiful." The tears poured from her. "How couldn't you want that for yourself? *I* want it. I want it with every fiber in my being, but I can't have it."

"Maeve—"

"But you can."

He reached out for her, but she pulled away.

"No. No, Jack. Don't. Don't make this any harder on me." She wiped the tears from her eyes and looked to the stars for strength, but they had become hidden by clouds. The darkness suited the moment, she thought abysmally. She could hide her pain in the darkness. "I won't have it, Jack. I can't look at a man I love every day of my life, knowing that I failed him. That I couldn't give him what he wanted. That he had to compromise to be with me."

"It's not like that. How could you even think that?"

Maeve wrapped her arms around herself. "One day Jack, you'll thank me for this. And when that day comes, I hope to God you'll be my friend again. Because I do love you. I love you so much, Jack."

"Let's just talk this through."

"Please, Jack. Please leave."

"I'm not leaving till we talk this over."

Maeve summoned the anger that was building inside her. Anger at the cancer. Anger at fate. Anger would give her enough strength to do what she knew needed to be done. "Then I'll leave."

She stormed up her back lawn to the house, just as the first raindrops fell.

CHAPTER 19

"Open up, Maeve!"

Maeve's eyes flew open and she looked at her clock. 11 a.m., it read. She wasn't surprised to have slept in, having cried all night. And the night before, for that matter.

The only thing that surprised her these days was that she had any tears left.

"Open up, Maeve, or I'm coming in. So you better be decent." Mick pounded on her door.

Decent? Maeve hadn't felt decent in forty-eight hours, barely emerging from her room. Turning off her iPhone. And not answering when Bess had told her Jack was trying to reach her.

She couldn't talk to him. Not yet. Her resolve was so tenuous, and she needed some space. Some time to remind herself of the reasons they couldn't be together.

Mick banged again, and Maeve buried her face in the pillow wishing he and Lacey had stayed in DC a little longer than two nights. Bess was hard enough to avoid. "Just come in," she finally told him. "It's not like it's locked, Mick."

He opened the door. "What the hell do you think you're doing, Maeve?"

"Trying to sleep, Mick. And good morning to you, too, Sunshine." She pulled the duvet over her head.

"Oh no, you don't." He sat on the bed and pulled the cover off her. "What the hell happened between you and Jack when we left?"

"I'm guessing you already know."

"Only what Bess told me, and she says you'll barely talk to her about it. She's worried. We all are."

"Jack never mentioned anything to you?" Why did that bother her so much? Maybe he had woken up the day after his proposal, grateful she had said no. He probably came to his senses, realizing that his life would be more complete without her.

Her shoulders sagged as she sank lower into the sheets. Maybe that's why he had been calling her yesterday. To tell her she had been right.

"He's a guy, Maeve. We don't share that crap. Besides, he doesn't even know we're back from DC yet."

"So? What else is there to say? He proposed. I turned him down. Game over." Her voice cracked as she said it.

"Only if you're stupid."

Maeve raised an unappreciative eyebrow. "Do you think maybe Lacey could be the one giving me the pep talk right now? Because you're not very good at it."

"Pep talk? You think that's why I'm in here?" He laughed. "Nope. It's payback time."

"Payback time?"

Mick crossed his arms. "About a year ago, you banged on my door at the crack of ass, waking my neighbors, and nearly causing an internal investigation at the Academy, all to tell me how stupid I was to let Lacey go."

She cocked her head, remembering. "You're exaggerating a little."

"Not a bit. People still talk about it. You attracted some serious attention that morning. But you got my attention, too. And you were right. Letting go of Lacey would have been the dumbest thing I could have done."

"And you think the same applies here?"

"Hell, yeah. If you're not ready to get married, that's fine. If you just want to date him longer, fine. But don't push him away because of some martyr bullshit."

"Bullshit?" Her eyes ignited with anger as she rose from her bed. "You call this bullshit? Me, not being able to have kids? Me, falling in love with someone who for two years has said nothing else except that he wants a family of his own? Do you know how much this hurts, Mick?" She wrapped her robe around her, arms aching, body shaking. Tears streaming from her eyes, she looked at herself in her armoire mirror and barely recognized herself. "What else could I do? Let him change his life plans just because of me?"

Mick stood next to her, gazing at her reflection in the mirror, letting the silence fill the room for longer than she had expected.

"Yeah," he finally said thoughtfully. "Yeah, I guess you're right."

She should have been happy he had conceded, but it pained her to hear it. "See?" she said, wiping her damp eyes on her robe's sleeve.

"Yeah, I guess if I found out Lacey couldn't have kids, I'd probably have to move on, too."

"*What?*"

Mick shrugged. "Having kids—that's a big deal. You get married and that's just kind of the expectation. I guess I can see what you mean."

"You son of a bitch!" A rage surged inside of her, and her fist flung, stopped only two inches from his face by his hand.

Mick's eyes flashed in triumph. "Aha! So you think it's okay for Jack, but not for me?" He released her hand. "Maeve, I don't give a rat's ass whether Lacey and I can have kids together or not. I married her because I want to spend the rest of my days with her. *Her.* Anyone else that comes into the picture later is a bonus." His eyes never left hers. "So why do I get to spend the rest of my life with the woman I love, and Jack doesn't?"

"He'd be happier without me."

"You really think that? Or is it just pride that's holding you back? You hold back on everything and everybody, don't you, Maeve? You didn't even tell us you'd had cancer because you like that feeling of being superior to us."

"Superior? It wasn't like that."

"Oh yes, it was. Perfect Maeve in her waterfront house with her BMW and more clothes than a woman could wear in a lifetime. Perfect Maeve who acted like men were little pets that you could take or leave. Perfect Maeve who couldn't trust that her friends loved her for *her*, not for her house or her shoes or her car. Or for this mask of perfection you wear." He paused with a grin. "Though I really do love your car."

She almost smiled at his last comment, but her mind flashed back over the past two years. "I never meant it that way," she said quietly.

"And now you're Perfect Maeve who won't marry Jack because it would make you feel flawed. You can't be flawed. Not you." He shook his head at her in the mirror. "Can't spend the rest of her life with someone who might think she's anything but perfect."

There was a quiet knock at the open door. Maeve glanced over to see Lacey.

Maeve narrowed her eyes. "It's about time you rescued me from this brute."

"From what I heard in the hall, I think he made some good points." She wrapped her arms around her friend.

Bess peeked in. "You okay?"

"Barely surviving," Maeve admitted.

"You should have called me," Lacey admonished, squeezing her tight.

"And disturb your mini honeymoon in DC? Never. How was it?"

"Magical. And a hell of a lot better than what's been going on here." Lacey held out her hand, dripping with borrowed jewels. "I have some jewelry to return." Her smile was timid.

"Thanks," Maeve said quietly.

"I'm so sorry about what happened. I wish you'd change your mind."

"Me too," Bess added. "I think you're making a huge mistake."

"What is this? An intervention?" Maeve smirked, taking Gram's necklace and earrings from Lacey's outstretched hand.

"I know you love him, Maeve. You're breaking his heart. And your own," Lacey reminded her.

"It's for the best, you guys." She lowered the jewelry into the box, briefly touching the medal from her Gram's lost love that rested at the bottom. "Jack will fall in love again. With someone right for him. More right than me."

Lacey reached for the medal that had caught Maeve's eye. "Like your grandma did?"

"Yeah."

"What's that?" Mick asked, reaching for the medal.

"Something of her grandma's," Lacey answered. "Maeve thinks it belonged to someone she loved before she married Maeve's grandfather."

Mick took it, flipped it over, and over again, and shrugged. "Not unless she was married in the last decade or so. This is pretty new."

Maeve looked at Mick. "What?"

"Yeah. The older ones have a different design. Not very different. But different enough. This is definitely recent. Looks the same as the one I got when I graduated from the Academy."

"Then who would it—?" Maeve's mind wandered to a weekend eight years ago. Buttons popping off uniforms. Pins falling to the floor…

And medals.

Oh dear Lord. She pressed her hand to her mouth. The medal was Jack's.

Jack must have lost it from his uniform that weekend after his graduation. Her grandmother had found it. Gram had known that Maeve had had a weekend fling while she was housesitting. And her grandmother had kept the medal all these years. *Why, Gram?*

Maeve's eyes flew out her bedroom door to the photo of her grandmother in the hall. "Destiny sometimes needs a push," she could almost hear Gram telling her.

Maeve thought back to the day her grandparents had returned from their trip. Maeve had been in an emotional haze, still glowing from the blissful 48 hours with Jack, but filled with regret that she had destroyed Jack's number. She had slapped on a smile for her grandparents, but Gram must have known something was wrong.

And then she had found the medal.

Gram had known her granddaughter had lost her heart to the man who lost this medal. And her grandmother had kept it, hoping that one day they would reunite.

My God. Maeve's eyes darted around her room, out to the hall, picturing every room in the house and the yard she had cherished these past two years. Was that why Gram had given Maeve the house? With the hope that she'd find him again, here in Annapolis?

It made perfect sense. Why else would Maeve have inherited the house rather than just letting it go into probate to be split between her and her brother?

So many questions, Maeve thought, gazing at the photo again, Gram's image reaching out to her from decades past.

Suddenly, Maeve knew the answers.

"Oh, Jack," she said quietly.

"What's wrong?" Lacey asked.

"Only everything." Maeve took the medal back from Mick and touched it to her lips. "Out. All three of you. I need to get dressed."

"Where are you going?" Bess walked backwards out the door.

"To give destiny a push."

Pride? Maeve pressed her foot against the accelerator as she sped across the Navy bridge. Above all the glaring realizations she had made that morning, she hated most figuring out that Mick was right.

He wasn't the type of man to let her forget it.

And she never would. Destiny had brought Jack back into her life, with maybe a nudge from Gram. Yet Maeve had stood there in the aftermath of a romantic wedding, beneath a rose-covered arbor she had built with Jack, and she had let pride stomp destiny into the grass beneath her.

Pride: 1. Destiny: 0.

Not any more.

She turned onto the quiet street that led to Jack's, giving a quick wave to little Grayson as he rode his bicycle in circles on his driveway. No lemonade stand today, she thought. And thank heaven, because she couldn't waste time stopping.

The movers had come this morning. Maeve didn't need the calendar on her iPhone to remember that. She had etched the day into her brain, dreading it for weeks. But with luck, she might catch him before they left.

In the distance she could see the house, but there were no trucks in front of it. No movers lugging furniture and boxes. The house was still.

He was gone.

Biting her lip, she pulled into the tucked-away driveway, now buried in fluffy hydrangeas. His truck peeked out at her from behind the leaves, sending a surge of anticipation down her spine, making her palms sweat.

She wasn't too late. Shutting her car door behind her, her steps toward his door slowed as her brain tried to find the right words. What *was* she here to say? She didn't really know. That she had been a fool. That she was lucky to have a man like him. That she wasn't nearly as healed from the battles she had fought as she had liked to think.

That he was her destiny.

Her hand rose to knock, but then froze. What if he had changed his mind? Maybe... but she still couldn't leave things the way they were.

Not knowing what she would say, she tapped on the door, lightly at first, then harder when he didn't answer. Again, she knocked and waited, as butterflies created havoc in her stomach.

But the house was quiet, so silent that she could hear the water lapping against the rocks and the hum of a boat or two as they powered down the Severn River.

Where was he? He couldn't have left without his truck.

She stepped into the backyard, and saw the hammock was gone. He'd hang it at his new home, she imagined, hoping she'd be able to see it first-hand. She pictured him for a moment, his strong legs dangling over the side of the hammock as he snoozed, an open book resting on his chest.

Standing in the center of the yard with her arms wrapped around her, she felt more alone at that moment than she had in two years.

Then she saw it—his red kayak on the other side of the Severn. From that distance, most men looked alike. But not Jack. She could make out his broad silhouette, his muscular arms moving the small craft swiftly across the water.

Running to the water's edge, she waved frantically. "Jack!" she called, but he didn't look her way. She cried out again, her voice swallowed up in the wind across the wide span of the Severn. "Jack!"

Again, no response. More desperate, she yelled louder. The neighbors would wonder, she was sure, and she was definitely attracting the attention of the boats that were anchored on her side of the river. "Jack!"

A sailor on one of them gave her a wave, and Maeve didn't even have the notion to feel mortified. "That guy?" he shouted, pointing to Jack's red kayak.

Maeve nodded. "Yes!" she called. "Thank you!"

He sounded his horn. Once. Then again.

Jack finally turned his head toward the sailboat. The sailor sounded his horn a third time and pointed to the shore where Maeve stood.

She called Jack's name, and her heart leapt when he raised his hand to her in recognition. He changed directions, giving a wave to the sailor as he passed the boat, and continued on toward Maeve.

At that moment when he was halfway across the Severn, when she could finally make out his eyes and a hint of worry in his expression, she knew what she had to say to him.

"Marry me, Jack Falcone!" she yelled. The words had flown from her mouth. All instinct, no pride, she finally would let her heart do the talking.

"What?" he called, as his kayak sliced through the water.

"Marry me!"

She saw his speed increase then, a wide grin flashing across his face and she knew. He still wanted her, faults and all.

He jumped from the kayak into the shallow water, pulling it close to the shoreline. "Did I hear you say what I think I heard you say?"

She stepped into the water without thinking, shoes still on, just to be closer to him. "I can't offer you all that I wish I could. But I know that I'll love you till the day I die." Hell with pride. She went down on one knee in the water, soaking herself to the bone. "Will you marry me, Jack Falcone?"

He thrust the kayak onto the shore and knelt in the water in front of her, taking her face in his palms. He said only one word before touching his lips to hers and changing their lives forever.

That word was "Yes."

FROM THE AUTHOR

Thank you so much for reading *The SEAL's Best Man*. If you enjoyed this book, I hope you will consider helping me spread the word by writing a review on Amazon. **Your reviews truly are the backbone of the low-budget marketing effort of an independent author like myself! So I am deeply grateful to you for your support**.

If you'd like me to let you know when my next book is ready, please contact me at my website at www.KateAster.com to get on my email list. Thanks for your interest!

ALSO WRITTEN BY KATE ASTER

Kate's most recent romance:

More, Please

And the continuation of the Special Ops: Homefront Series:

SEAL the Deal
Special Ops: Homefront (Book One)

Contract with a SEAL
Special Ops: Homefront (Book Three)

Make Mine a Ranger
Special Ops: Homefront (Book Four)

New books are on their way! You can stay updated at:

www.KateAster.com

Made in the USA
Lexington, KY
12 December 2017